MUTILATED

Mississippi's Most Hated Cannibal

A novel By

AMANDA LEE

INTRODUCTION

REAGUS DUNE is my name, and I'm a known cannibal. I was violent with my kills. It didn't matter whom I killed just to taste the human flesh. After the first taste of eating my baby sister, I was hooked. I terrified the streets of Forest, Mississippi, hunting down my prey one by one, eating. My passion to murder and dismember each prey with my bare hands was so great. People went to the grocery store to eat. I went to the streets. Killing humans was my second job. I wanted to taste them deep inside me.

Some had a unique smell, and I loved the aroma coming from their flesh. Others tasted horrible, tainted. I knew one day, I would get caught, but that didn't stop me from slaughtering and eating the human flesh. Being sentenced to life in prison was like a dream come true, until I began killing back-to-back, eating.

Instead of life in prison, I was sentenced to DEATH.

CHAPTER 1

(Violent Behavior)

A prison fight erupted, and inmates cheered, as three others attacked me. They were beating me senselessly until I wrestled the smallest one down, sinking my teeth into his neck and devouring a piece. The other two slowly stepped back, scared and shocked. Chewing meat, blood gargled in the inmate's throat, and his body trembled. A tear escaped from his left eye with a dead stare at the ceiling, mouth wide, blood trickling down onto the floor.

"What the hell?" the inmate covered with tattoos stated, as he prepared to kick me.

"Oh, shit!" the other inmate screamed, both stepping back.

I couldn't resist pulling his esophagus from his neck with my teeth. The smell of his body was overpowering. The inmate began convulsing, as if having a seizure. I began biting, devouring more flesh. Glancing down, blood spurted from his neck into my face, almost blinding me. Swallowing, I bit him again and again until the Emergency Response Team rushed through the prison doors, demanding everyone go back into their cells. I didn't move; I just kept eating.

"Lock it down!" Captain Dalton yelled, as the doors were closing shut.

"What the fuck?" Officer Keyes spoke with a taser pointed at the front of my forehead.

"He's eating him," Officer Combs called out.

"Take that mutherfucker out," Captain Dalton demanded, as two officers hit me with tasers.

Electricity hit me so hard. My knees wobbled for a few seconds, pulling the prongs from my body. Standing tall, I jumped up, screaming and beating on my chest like King Kong. The prison fell silent, as my screams rang throughout the prison.

"Fuck," Officer Combs screamed out.

"Hit him again," Captain Dalton yelled.

Scanning the officers, I scouted the weakest link. Rushing him, I took him down to the ground, hitting him repeatedly until I was dazed again with another taser. Falling onto the ground, I shook like a seizure patient. Pulling the prongs from my body again, I stood to my feet. Before I could do anything, an officer hit me with a tranquilizer dart in my neck. Pulling the dart from my neck, I dropped flat on my face.

"Lights out, mutherfucker." Captain Dalton smirked. He continued, "Drag his ass out and take him to lockdown."

Officer Combs helped Officer Keyes to his feet, as two other officers grabbed me by the feet, dragging me to lockdown like a rag doll.

Sitting in the lock for a week, I became delusional and hungry. I craved my favorite meat. In my mind, the next officer who came through that door was dead. But…

"Captain Dalton, get in here now," Officer Keyes radioed, as he looked through the plastic window of the cell.

"What's wrong, Keyes? Stop acting like a pussy!" Captain Dalton radioed back, laughing.

"We have a situation with Dune."

"What situation?"

"He's eating his flesh, blood everywhere," Officer Keyes stated with a disgusted look on his face.

Sitting there, chewing my flesh, I smiled at him. The Emergency Response Team came down in full force on my Black ass. By the looks of it, they were coming to take my life.

"What the hell are you doing, Dune?" Captain Dalton stated, as he opened the door, and officers rushed in with tranquilizer guns. They all had their guns aimed at me, so I decided not to move. I wanted to be awake for whatever they were going to do to me.

"He's eating his flesh," Officer Keyes stated.

"No shit, Sherlock. I can see that," Captain Dalton shot back with a blank expression.

"Dune, get your ass up. If you try anything, you're going down. With all these tranquilizers, I doubt if you ever wake up," Captain Dalton threatened.

"Fuck you, Dalton," I stated, as I stood up slowly, very exhausted.

"Keep talking shit, I'll leave your Black ass down here to die."

"It doesn't matter. I'm going to die anyway," I remarked, as I rushed Dalton, taking his old ass down to the ground. Suddenly, I felt a sting on my back. My body lost control, falling over. Dalton used his leg to kick me over onto the floor.

"That boy isn't going to learn," Officer Combs said, as he looked at the gun he'd just discharged.

"You should have known he was going to try something. This is every single time we deal with his ass," Officer Keyes stated.

"Shut up, Keyes, with your scared ass. He almost made you shit on yourself last time," Captain Dalton sarcastically spoke.

"Whatever." Officer Keyes frowned.

"Don't whatever me. Get this clown out of here to medical," Captain Dalton ordered. Keyes and Combs grabbed my feet, dragging me to medical, leaving a blood trail.

Two more weeks passed, and those dirty mutherfuckers had my arm wrapped, blood seeping through the bandage, and I was chained up like an animal. Both arms were chained to the wall, as I stood on my feet. My legs were exhausted, and I fell to my knees. They fed me whenever they desired. An officer would come into the cell, place my dinner plate and a cup of water at my feet, then unlock one arm. Once I finished, two officers came in, one with a tranquilizer gun aimed directly at my head, and the other locked my arm back up. The look in that officer's eyes who held the gun showed he was dead serious about his job. I just stared at him each time he came in, letting him know that I wasn't scared to die.

Walking down the hall, officers had me chained from head to toe. I had a face mask that connected to the chain around my neck. The neck chain was connected to wrist chains, and they were connected to a waist chain. The waist chain was connected to ankle chains. They had me chained like an armed and dangerous killer.

They marched me down the hall like soldiers with shotguns ready to blow my head off. As we speedwalked, I stared at the freshly painted gray walls and shiny white floors. There were no windows present. It had been a year or more since I saw daylight.

Stopping at this room, they unlocked the

door, and I stepped in. There were more gray walls and white floors. There stood a psychiatrist, Amanda Smith. She was a thick, white girl with long, blonde hair, pedicured nails, and toes covered with pink polish. Her white dress with pink flowers caught my eye, but her overpowering smell almost knocked me down. This was a girl I would devour in a few hours for sure.

"Why is he chained like that?" Dr. Smith frowned, as a green vein appeared on her forehead, and her hands went on her hips.

"This is for your protection and ours. Dune is extremely dangerous and will kill you in seconds," Captain Dalton spoke, as he appeared behind us.

"At least remove the face mask. You have him looking like Hannibal Lecter," she shot back.

"Hannibal Lector. Don't compare me to that idiot. I'm cleverer than he is," I stated, as the officers sat me down at the table far from Dr. Amanda Smith.

"You can't be too clever because you're locked up," Dr. Smith shot back, as she put her hand over her mouth.

"You're one of those," I spoke, as I was chained down.

Officers stood behind me with shotguns. They were overreacting, but of course, I loved my favorite meat. Dr. Smith smelled just like Bonnie Logan. I almost fainted.

"My apologies," Dr. Smith said.

"Get on with this so-called interview," I said.

"Okay then, let's see."

"Why are you nervous?" I asked.

"I'm not nervous, just can't find my notebook."

"I'm not going to hurt you. These officers are here for a reason. Plus, I'm chained up. No need in being nervous," I said, as she continued to fumble around in her briefcase.

Officer Keyes lifted his gun, pointing at me. Dr. Smith's eyes got big. Officer Combs nodded to her.

"You know you smell like her," I stated, as I sniffed into the air.

"Smell like who?" she asked with a faint smile.

"Bonnie Logan," I replied.

"That's your very first victim, correct?" she asked, as she stopped in her tracks, staring me down.

"I wouldn't call her my first victim because I didn't get a chance to devour her. I only tasted her."

"Why her?" Dr. Smith asked, as she pulled her notebook out and sat down to take notes.

"She smelled so delicious; I couldn't resist. She smelled like you."

"Do you want to eat me?"

"Yes.'

Officer Keyes lifted his gun, as he looked at Officer Combs. Officer Combs nodded his head. Officer Keyes looked nervous, but I knew he would blow my head off in a second with no hesitation.

"Too bad. I'm not available to be eaten."

"I know, but you sure as hell could taste good. Your pretty skin, your long, blonde hair. I would have to cut off your hair and scalp you. I'd probably bust your head open with a hammer over and over until your skull cracks open," I explained with a smile.

"Cool it, Dune," Officer Combs ordered.

"The doctor asked me a question, and I answered. That's why I am here to be interviewed. Isn't that right, Doc?" I spoke.

"You're correct, Mr. Dune," Dr. Smith replied.

"That's my so-called father's name. Call me Reagus or call me nothing at all," I stated.

"Okay, Reagus it is," Dr. Smith replied.

"Are you sure you're not Bonnie Logan?"

"I'm very sure I'm not Bonnie Logan. My parents are from New York. I don't have any relatives down here in Mississippi," Dr. Smith said.

"Back to me killing you. I think I would bust your head open with one crack of a hammer," I stated.

"One more time and you're going back to lockdown," Officer Keyes said harshly.

"I'm just playing with Doc. I would probably rip out her insides." I laughed, as Dr. Smith shifted in her seat.

"Can we begin the interview?" Dr. Smith interrupted.

"Sure, whenever you're ready," I replied, as I continued to sniff the air.

Dr. Amanda Smith asked, "What incidents occurred to you in the East Mississippi Mental Institution as a child that has caused you to be violent? There is something that triggered you inside to torture your victims, making them suffer."

"I suffered in that place, and nobody wanted to help me because I was that person that liked to eat people. You have no idea about the incidents that I suffered. There is no worse feeling in the world than being sodomized at the age of ten. My first night was a living hell. I had a broken leg. I grew up in a hostile environment. Those so-called staff members you all have taught me extreme violence. You want to call them incidents. I call them torture. I don't want to talk about this anymore. If you continue to talk about it, I will leave this interview," I answered.

Dr. Amanda Smith spoke, "Okay, I will move on. So, why did you skin and scalp two of your victims?"

"You mean why did I start skinning and scalping my prey? There were only two. What intrigued my mind to commit such a beautiful crime was when I had this beautiful Indian girl stalk me. She followed me everywhere, so it was natural for me to get rid of her, so others could die. I couldn't let her stop me from eating my favorite meat. She stalked me for about three months. And the other girl was because I was curious how she would taste. She had that special smell I loved, but her skin was super dark. Her heritage was African. A very dark-skinned girl but her smell was sweeter than usual. That African girl had to die a gruesome death."

Occurred Incidents: SCALPING THE PREY
THE FIRST PREY

"Why are you following me everywhere I go?" I snapped, walking up to this Indian girl named Victoria Sophie. She was a halfway pretty girl, but I wasn't interested in her.

"I don't mean to be rude. I find you incredibly attractive," Victoria spoke softly while presenting a huge smile that displayed her crooked teeth.

"That's very annoying, having you follow me like that. What do you want from me?"

"I want to be your friend and hopefully, if you like me, a little more, as in a girlfriend." She smiled again, as I grinded my teeth.

"Girlfriend? You can't be serious. I don't find you attractive at all. You have crooked teeth with a big nose. Girls like you should be somewhere hiding." I laughed, as her face went from happy to sad. I continued, "Go on and get out of here."

"I didn't realize you were so rude. I thought you were a different and unique person. Thank you for showing me the real you." She softly spoke with tears forming in her eyes, walking up to me.

Victoria stood in front of me, causing my nose to open wide. Taking a step closer to her, I took a deeper sniff of her hair. She jerked away immediately. Looking at me eye-to-eye, tears rolled down Victoria's face. I lifted a finger to rub her wet, crying face, and she embraced my touch. Pulling her close to me, I embraced her, as I closed my eyes and took in my favorite smell. It was like Victoria had me in a deep trance. Smelling her was almost unbearable for me to manage while standing in front of the Brackeen-Wood Gymnasium.

Almost losing myself in her, I snapped back to reality when a couple of girls from the softball team passed by, laughing. I opened my eyes and gave them an evil look. Pulling Victoria away, I stated, "Would you like to go to my house and talk?"

"Yes, I would love that." She sniffled, as she looked at me.

"Great, my car is over there in the parking lot." I pointed, as I grabbed her hand, leading her to my car.

"Would it be okay if I drove my car? I don't want you to go out of your way to bring me back to school," Victoria asked.

"I don't mind bringing you back to school. Just leave your car here because it will be a waste of gas just driving back and forward. Plus, if you decide to stay the night, I have an extra room you can stay in," I lied, as I knew once she left with me, she would never return alive.

"Are you sure?" she asked again.

Pulling her toward my car, I nodded my head, not speaking a word. She followed me with no hesitation. Hitting the car lock and unlocking the door for her, I scanned my surroundings, making sure that nobody saw me. A few boys were standing out, but I didn't think they noticed us.

Closing the car door, I rushed over to the driver's side, cranking the car and driving off.

"Are you sure about me not taking my car, Reagus?" Victoria asked me one last time.

"Stop asking me the same question over and over. I said I don't mind bringing you back to school," I snapped before I realized it.

"Wait, stop the car. I changed my mind," Victoria spoke with a worried look on her face. I ignored her and kept driving.

"I'm sorry for snapping at you. I just hate being asked the same thing over and over. As I mentioned before, I don't mind bringing you back to school. I do have to come back to class tomorrow."

"If you don't mind, I would like to come back tonight."

"You have a curfew?" I asked, hoping that she did not.

"No, I don't have a curfew. It's kind of strange."

"How so?" I asked.

"Usually, I am following your car around everywhere, and now, I am in the car with you. This has been a dream come true for me," Victoria explained, as I sped down the back road through Conehatta to get to my house.

"I noticed that you were following me everywhere. You even know where I live. Have you ever brought anyone out here to my house?" I asked.

"No, I have never. I have always followed you by myself. I know everything there is to know about you," she admitted. That statement alone was creepy. I never knew a girl would stalk me.

"You know that sounds scary." I laughed.

"I know, but I have fallen in love with you," she stated, as I looked over at her and almost wrecked. This girl was something serious.

"Falling in love with me. That's a mighty big statement."

"Yes, it is, but it is the truth. I want to belong to you and no one else."

"And you say this is a dream come true for you. Well, I will make tonight special, just for you. I promise I won't harm you or do anything you don't want me to. Tonight, will be about me and you," I replied, as I continued to drive the rest of the way to my house. No words were spoken, just silence.

Arriving at the black gates, I unlocked them from the outside, pulled my car through, then secured them behind me. I wanted to make sure that no one disturbed me.

Driving up to the house, Victoria's eyes had gotten so big. She was taking in everything she saw for memories. "Is everything okay?"

"Yes, Reagus. I was just admiring the exterior of your beautiful home. I always loved the red tin roof. When it rains, you can hear it beating, trying to get in. That is some good sleep," Victoria remarked, as she opened the car door and began walking to the front door. I had to jump out and catch up to her.

"Hold on, girl. You are walking mighty fast. You're walking as if you're familiar with my property," I stated.

"No, I haven't invaded your privacy. The farthest I have gone is the front gate, where you keep it locked." She smiled.

Opening the front door to let her in, she walked as if she was familiar with my house. Victoria stopped in the living room and began undressing. I didn't say a word at first but watched. She stood in front of me, naked, and the aroma coming off her was appealing again.

"Take me, Reagus. I belong to you now," Victoria remarked, as I continued to stare at her nicely shaped body. Her breasts were perkier than I thought. Her stomach was flat, as if she had been working out at the gym, and her calf muscles were nice.

"Wow. You have a very nice body," I managed to say, as my eyes began to roll in the back of my head, and she walked over to me. Her smell was killing me. I fell to my knees, as she approached me and pushed my face into her sweet vagina. It was bald and full of aroma. I began kissing her, and suddenly, I bit down with my teeth, as she began to scream. I put my hand over her mouth and twisted her head.

Pushing my head backward, I bit harder and shook my head like a pit bull. Finally, after ripping off a piece of her flesh, she fell to the floor, still screaming. Her hands covered my damage, as I chewed her flesh, looking at her. Blood dripping down my chin, I quickly bit down on her side until I pulled another piece of meat. Her screams were more traumatizing than I had imagined. She tried to get up, and I punched her in the face. She kept coming at me, so I punched her two more times. I had knocked Victoria out cold.

Picking her body up off the floor, I carried her into my back bedroom. That was where I prepared for my first victim to be scalped. I tied Victoria up to the bed frame quickly because she was beginning to wake up. After becoming fully awake, her face filled with fear, as tears formed in her eyes.

"Please let me go. I promise I won't tell the police," Victoria stated, as she tried to get her hands out of the restraints, I placed her in.

"We are beyond that, little Ms. Victoria. I hadn't planned on killing you, but I couldn't have you sneaking around here either. You should have stayed away and disappeared from my life, but now, you must die for it," I replied with a smirk on my face.

"You're going to kill me. I don't deserve this." She sobbed, as she continued to try to get out of the restraints.

"You do deserve to die. You know it's a crime to stalk people, and that's what you did to me. You have invaded my privacy. But of course, this isn't about you stalking me. This is about that unique smell coming from your body." I sniffed, leaning in to get a better smell. Blood leaked on the floor that was coming from her side.

I couldn't stop myself, so I now bit in her other thigh, pulling away her flesh like a mad dog. Bite after bite, she screamed for her dear life, begging me to stop eating off her flesh.

"Victoria, my darling, you can stop screaming because no one can hear you. I know you have realized how deep in the woods my house is. So, you can stop yelling," I spoke, as I stood up and walked away. It was time to start scalping her. I had to experience it.

"Reagus, I don't want to die. Please don't kill me. Do whatever you want, just please don't kill me," Victoria begged.

"Too late, my dear. You are sentenced to death," I replied, as I opened the closet and pulled out my vibrating saw. As I turned on the electrical device, Victoria began to beg me more and more, as I walked toward her.

"Reagus, no," she screamed.

"Shut up and die like a champ," I remarked, as I straddled her body.

I pulled her hair back tight, as I had seen on YouTube videos, and I began chipping away at her flesh, as it peeled back like an onion. Cut by cut, I removed all her hair. I just ripped the rest like I was tearing up paper. The screams from her mouth were unbearable. She gave me a headache. Holding her scalp in my hand and tossing it to the floor, I began chipping away at her flesh where I had bitten.

After skinning her alive, Victoria's voice was almost gone. I turned off the saw and began eating her alive right there. I ate and ate until I was almost sick. By this time, she was almost dead. Reaching into her stomach, I ripped out her guts. Her eyes were placed on the ceiling without a blink, and tears escaped from her eyes. It was official. Victoria was dead.

After killing Victoria, I sawed the rest of her body up and placed my meat into Zip-loc bags. Cutting off her head, feet, and hands, I placed them into a garbage bag to prepare for later. But first, I had to clean up my mess and shower.

Putting on fresh clothes, I went down by the black gate surrounding my property and began digging a hole for my plant. I had decided that after killing each person, I was going to bury their head, feet, hands, and the rest of the torso under my favorite plant and call it the "red rock crape" tree. After digging a not-so-big hole, I went back to the house and retrieved the remains of Victoria's body, so I could bury it. Collecting my red rock crape tree, I headed back down to the black gate. Dumping her head, feet, hands, and torso in the hole, I covered it with dirt. Placing a little Miracle Grow there too, I planted my red rock crape tree. Victoria was my first victim.

THE SECOND PREY

Heading back home after school, I spotted this very dark-skinned African girl walking along Highway 21. I recognized her from school but didn't want to stop. It was late in the evening, but I smiled to myself and stopped.

"Excuse me, Miss, it's kind of late out here. Can I give you a ride?" I asked, as I stopped next to her.

"No, thank you." She sobbed, as she continued to walk slowly. I hadn't noticed she was crying until she spoke.

"Please, ma'am, I don't like seeing women like this," I lied, as I pulled in front of her and jumped out of the vehicle.

"Don't you come near me," she yelled, waving a huge knife. Her body was tiny and fragile. She looked like she had been crying for a long time. She had bags under her eyes, and her skin was so smooth.

"Whoa! I am just trying to help you. I promise I won't harm you. I recognized you from

East Central Community College and decided to stop. I am not here to cause problems," I replied, as I acted like I feared her and her knife. I could have taken her down quickly in the state she was in.

"I'm sorry, but do I know you?"

"No, you don't know me, but I have seen you around the college with the girls from the softball team."

"Probably so, but I don't play softball. One of the girls is my roommate, and she plays."

"Great, see, I have seen you at school before. Now, can I please help you? I see that you've been crying, and out here by yourself is not good. You don't know what kind of people come up and down Highway 21," I stated but didn't bother to snitch on myself. I was one of those people who was ready to kill her off and never think about it again.

"My boyfriend and I were arguing about him dumping me for another girl. He got me out of the car and drove off. I didn't think he was going to leave me out here. I have been walking for about two hours now, trying to get back to Sebastopol," she stated, as more tears escaped her eyes.

"I live in Sebastopol. I don't mind giving you a ride home. Where exactly do you stay?"

"I live in Sebastopol Apartments. How far do you live from there?" she asked.

"My residence is at the corner of Highway 21 and West Street. I moved there about two months ago. Everyone thinks it is a creepy spot, but it's okay so far. No ghosts there lol," I joked, as I reached out to grab her hand.

Looking at my extended hand, she gave me her hand. Opening the passenger door to let her in, her immaculate smell slapped me in the face. Falling to my knees, I lost my balance.

"Oh, my, what's wrong?" she asked, as she grabbed me and helped me back to my feet.

"My knee gave out on me," I lied again. Her smell was so strong that it knocked me off my feet.

"Does that happen often?"

"No, this was the first time that ever happened."

"Are you sure you can drive the both of us home?" she asked with a smile on her face. Her tears had disappeared.

"I am very sure," I assured her, as I straightened myself and walked around the vehicle to get in the driver's side. I took a deep breath before I got in. Her smell was going to kill me all the way there.

"And you're okay to drive?" she asked again.

"Yes, ma'am, I am sure I can drive. What is your name? My name is Reagus."

"My name is Ode Bahati Ekon, but everyone calls me Odie."

"Okay, Odie, nice to meet you."

"Nice to meet you, Reagus." She laughed, as I drove off.

We talked about school and how she came to America. As we passed Jackson Road, I told her that my grandparents had left me a house out there. My thoughts immediately went to Bonnie Logan from school. I had moved to Sebastopol because of her, so I wanted to get close to her. She worked at Sebastopol Attendance Center as a teacher, but I didn't tell Odie all that.

"Why don't you just live in the house that your grandparents gave you instead of renting this old house on the corner?" Odie asked.

"Because I am thinking about working at Sebastopol Clinic and wanted to get closer to my job. That's why I decided to get an associate's degree in nursing at EC," I explained.

"Nursing. I wouldn't have imagined that." She giggled while placing her hand over her mouth like a small child who was scared to show their smile.

"What's wrong with nursing?"

"Nothing is wrong with it. I thought you were going to say that you're a football player or something else the way your body is structured," Odie stated, as she undressed me with her eyes.

"No, ma'am, definitely not a football player." I smiled back.

"Nursing is a good career. My parents wanted me to become a doctor, but I love music more. They won't even talk to me about it, so I went ahead and changed my major to music."

"Music is okay. You're trying to be a singer or rapper?" I joked.

"Unfortunately, I am not a rapper, but I do love to sing. The melody takes me into another world. This world is so cruel," Odie stated, as she got quiet and began staring out the window. I didn't say another word but drove her home.

All the way there, I wanted to stop and kill her off. Nobody would miss her. Her family, maybe, but they were in another country. By the time they reported her missing, I would have eaten her by then.

Pulling up at Sebastopol Apartments, I let her out. She walked around and gave me a big hug. Her smell was so overwhelming. She was so small and fragile that I was sure I could kill her with one blow to the temple. There was one nosey, light-skinned, Black female sitting outside looking, so I hugged Odie and left without my favorite meat. This was the first time that I ever met someone with such a strong odor that I didn't kill.

I thought, There is no way in hell I am letting that Odie girl live. That was the second time *my knees ever collapsed on me from an overpowering smell. The smell of her flesh was so overpowering, and it made me feel weak. I can't be around her; she must die. Still thinking about Odie, I finally dozed off until I heard a knock at my door.*

Looking at my watch, it was 2 a.m. Who in the hell was at my door? I knew that people who lived in Sebastopol would not come to my home besides the police. "Oh, shit," I whispered, as I walked to the door and opened it.

"Hey, Reagus," a small, sweet voice whispered, as I looked out at her. I didn't say anything at first because of the unique smell of her flesh hitting me in the face. Snapping back to reality, I managed speaking.

"What are you doing here?" I asked without inviting her in.

"I'm so sorry for intruding on you like this, but I need to talk to you. Are you alone?" she asked, trying to peep around me.

"Yes, I'm alone."

"Can I please come in?" Odie stated in such a way that caused my knees to get weak again. As I fell to the ground, Odie rushed up to help me. Falling backward, I tried to restrain myself from killing her in my doorway.

Odie stepped over to me, as she closed the front door. I just lay there, as she stood over me. "Reagus, are you okay?"

"Yes, I am just fine. Just get back."

"What's wrong with you? This is the second time that you have collapsed like this," Odie stated, as she sat down on the floor where I continued to lay.

"Yes, Odie. It's just that you have this unique smell about you, and it makes me weak just talking to you," I honestly told her.

"My smell?" she replied, as she sniffed herself and continued. "Sorry, we don't believe in deodorant."

"Maybe," I spoke, as I finally sat up, shaking my head.

"Reagus, I want you. After you dropped me off at home, you have been on my mind," Odie stated, as she crawled over to me and climbed in my lap.

Odie pulled off her thin shirt, exposing her very dark-skinned breasts. The sight of them caused me to almost vomit. I began gagging, causing her to jump off me. Gathering myself to my feet quickly, I grabbed her by the neck, almost snapping it in half.

"You're hurting me," she called out, as I gripped her tightly.

"Why are you over here? Are you here to kill me?" I shouted.

"No, I'm not here to harm you in any type of way. Nobody knows that I have walked over to your house," she explained.

"You just walked over here without anybody knowing where you are?" I replied, as I released her neck.

"Yes. I just wanted to see you and offer my body. You turn me on." Odie smiled and turned away like she was shy. Still smiling, she grabbed the crotch of my pants, stroking me. I didn't push her away this time. Just stood there as she stroked my bone.

"I don't know if I should be doing this. This isn't what I want from you."

"What do you want from me, Reagus? You know you want me just as bad as I want you."

"I want you but not in the way you're thinking."

"How so?"

"You will find out soon enough. Just please stop," I stated.

"Are you a virgin?" Odie asked with a smirk on her face.

"Are you?" I smarted off back to her. She grinned at me, shaking her head in the no position.

As she stroked me, my bone was limp. Grabbing her shoulders, I motioned for her to get on her knees. Unzipping my pants, Odie pulled down my pants and underwear. My nine-inch stick lay flat. Placing her mouth on me, I immediately grew long. It was throbbing so badly, and I didn't want it to respond to her kind, but it did. As she sucked and pulled my bone, I ejaculated right there in her face. It exploded like no other, and I was embarrassed. As soon as she released me, I dropped to the floor and lay there.

"That was quick. I hope you have energy for round two," she stated, as she grabbed it again, and I pushed her away.

"Don't touch me. Just don't touch me," I managed to get out. I had never let anyone of her kind touch me like that before. I was just disgusted with myself. My body wasn't supposed to react to her like that.

Odie turned away from me as if she was offended. As soon as she turned around to face me, I hit her as hard as I could in the face with my fist. Her fragile body fell to the floor very hard. The blow to her face didn't knock her out, but it dazed her. Standing on my feet, I took my foot, kicking her multiple times in the head, knocking her out cold.

I looked down at her motionless body and thought, You should have never come over here. I was going to let you live for a few more days. And now, you're here at my house, looking stupid. How pathetic of you to think I wanted sex from you? Your body is not of my kind. I just wanted the beautiful meat you offered.

Coming out of my thoughts, I immediately tied her up and stuffed her into my truck. I had to take her body to Slaughter's Den. That was my *place on Patrick Drive in Steeletown. All my relatives from the country were asleep.*

As I pulled up down the dark, dirt road, Odie began to wake up. She was trying to scream through the black Gorilla Tape I'd placed over her mouth. Closing the black gate and pulling up to the barn doors, I jumped out with excitement. Opening the back door on my truck, it reeked of urine. Odie had pissed on herself. I immediately became angry, as I grabbed her by her hair and snatched her out of my truck. Her tied-up body fell to the hard, cold ground.

"Shit, Odie, you pissed on my carpet," I yelled, as I grabbed her by the hair and pulled her into the barn. She was trying to struggle through the tape. Looking back at her as I pulled her body, fear filled her eyes. Smiling, I was proud of myself.

Odie's body lay on the barn floor, as I prepared for her. Hanging already from my ceiling were two bloody ropes I had used before in a killing. I tied the rope around each of her ankles and then cut the Gorilla Tape to relieve her. Odie started trying to move around like a wounded animal. Grabbing the other end of the ropes, I began pulling her tired body up toward the ceiling, stringing her up like a dead reindeer being prepared for mutilation.

After hanging her body, I walked over, grabbing my large scissors to cut off her pants. As I began cutting her clothes from her body, she was trying to speak through the Gorilla Tape again, probably begging for her life, but it fell on deaf ears. Trying my best not to harm my favorite meat, her clothing was finally off. She was naked, and the smell was just too much for me. Falling to the ground and looking at her, I had to overcome her unique smell. My body had never reacted this way to the smell. But the unique smell of her flesh was overpowering and loud. My mouth was watery, ready to eat every inch of her.

Gathering myself, I took a flashlight and examined her body. Her back had so many scars. My meat was damaged. "You tricked me; you tricked me." I began to scream. Odie was violently shaking her head. Pulling my hair and screaming at myself loudly, I ran over to my Louisville Slugger baseball bat I had in the corner. Picking it up, I ran back over to her while holding the bigger end in my hand. Just standing there with disappointment on my face, I dropped the bat and then grabbed the scissors again to cut the tape from her mouth. I wanted to hear her scream, as I beat the life from her ugly body.

Cutting her face open, I pulled the tape from around her mouth, releasing her sound. "Please don't kill me. Please."

"Shut up, Odie, just shut up."

"Reagus, please don't kill me." She burst out into a full-blown scream.

"Shut up," I yelled again. I picked up the bat and began pounding away at the ugly scars on her back. Odie screamed with pain, as I crushed her spine into pieces. Every time my bat touched her skin, you could hear the spine cracking. As I hit her repeatedly, there were no more screams. Odie was lifeless.

Falling to the ground with the bat still in my hand, I just stared at the barn wall. I'd damaged the meat even more with my bad temper. "Damn it, Reagus Dune. You are stupid."

I thought, What if I don't want this meat now because of the damage I have caused? But the smell is even greater than her death. Just eat her, Reagus. Stop playing around and just eat the bitch.

Standing tall, I pulled this silver foot tub bucket over and placed it under her body. I had to collect blood for my favorite bottles of wine. Getting a sharp blade, I began skinning the scars from her body. Slicing across the lower part of her back, I began slicing the skin off her back. After cutting the scarred skin from her back to her shoulder blade, I ripped the skin from her body.

Suddenly, Odie's eyes popped open. She didn't move or anything but just had a blank stare. I didn't care about that, so I continued to slice pieces of her meat and toss it onto a nearby table. After a few minutes of cutting, I placed my hand on her bald vagina and turned her body around to her buttocks. Biting into her ass, I pulled chunks of meat from her and devoured it. I didn't stop until I ate all her ass.

Taking off my shirt, I continued to slaughter her. I decapitated her head from her body then tossed it on the ground along with the hands I had severed from her body. After that, I dropped her body to the ground. Cutting off her feet, I tossed them over by her head and hands. Taking an axe to her corpse, I had to separate her at the joints to grow my red rock crape tree.

I stopped to think for a minute. I should have scalped her head and cleaned the skull. Then, I could use the eyeballs for my chocolate-covered cherries. There was so much that I could do with her body parts but decided to let it go. There would be others.

As I stuffed her mutilated body into a garbage bag, I grabbed a red rock crape tree, a single bag of Miracle Grow, and an axe from the barn and headed down by the black gate. There were so many trees already planted. Moving about twelve inches apart from the last tree, I began digging a huge hole to bury Odie's body and plant my tree. After I completed digging my hole, I poured the mutilated body into the hole first then Miracle Grow on top. Covering the hole, I then

*planted my red rock crape tree. Another body was
down with many more to go.*

CHAPTER 2

(First Complete Meal)

Dr. Amanda Smith asked, "Tell me about the first time you tasted human flesh, and how did you feel afterward?"

"Tasting the flesh of that little white girl was immaculate. Her name was Bonnie Logan. She had this unique smell about her. That's what attracted me to her," I answered, as I sniffed in the air, trying to recapture the peculiar smell. I closed my eyes and remembered my first taste.

Occurred Incident: FIRST VICTIM

I sat down on this old, rusty swing set on the school playground, watching Bonnie Logan, as she ran around, playing with a couple of other children. Each time she passed by me, that smell just took over my nose. It was like I was in a trance, just sniffing like a dog. Finally, she and the others stopped, turning their attention toward me. I knew at that moment they were about to start picking at me like they did every day. They would call me nasty and pick at my clothes. My mother couldn't afford name-brand clothing, so I had to wear pants with holes in them, my shirt was filthy with dirt, and my left shoe had a hole in the toe, showing my foot.

*It was the worst thing I could have ever
experienced.*

*There was nothing more embarrassing than
being bullied. But that was not why I started eating
people. It was an immaculate smell. It was a unique,
strange smell. Maybe a mixture of burnt flesh and
peaches. The explanation of the smell is irrelevant,
just to say it was an odd smell I could not get out of
my nostrils.*

*Moving on. I watched Bonnie Logan every
single day, but on July 17, 2004, it was different.
My cravings became so unbearable that I couldn't
let another day go without tasting her. Recess was
over with, and it was time to go inside. We all lined
up, and Bonnie said she left her hair bow on the
playground. The teacher directed her to go get it,
and the others entered the building, heading to the
classroom. I stood at the door and told Mrs. White
that I would hold the door until Bonnie came in. She
didn't say anything but nodded and went behind the
class. They all disappeared into the classroom.
Bonnie retrieved her bow and ran toward the door.
I stepped outside, letting the door close. It
automatically locked behind me. Bonnie pulled on
the door and began to criticize me as always. I
knew at that moment; it was my time to taste her
flesh. She was smelling extra loud that day, and I
had to taste it. Today was my day to taste human
flesh.*

"You big dummy. The door is locked. How are we going to get in now?" she snapped, as she pulled on the door again.

"I'm not a dummy," I said, as I pushed her down with force that I didn't realize I had.

"You are a nasty dog. How dare you push me?"

Before she could say another word, I jumped down on her and began choking her. She started crying and scratching my hands around her neck, gasping for air. I released my grip from her neck then lifted her dress, biting down on her small, white, fragile thigh. Her screams filled the air, as I moved my head backward and forward like a pit bull, trying to tear a piece of her flesh. After tearing at her flesh, a large chunk of meat broke free, and my mouth was filled with meat and blood. I sat back and tried to chew fast. She cried and cried out. After I swallowed quickly, I jumped on her again and took out another big chunk of her thigh. As I sat up, Mrs. White was rushing through the door with two other teachers.

I sat back, looking up at all of them, while chewing my meat and blood running down my mouth onto my dirty shirt. Mrs. White reached down and picked up Bonnie like a wounded animal and ran into the building. Both teachers just stood there, looking at me. I spoke, "She tastes really good, just like I imagined."

The whole community was shattered, and Forest Elementary banned me from coming back. My mother came to the school that day and beat me over and over, while the principal and other teachers watched. They stood by and did nothing, as that crackhead beat me unconscious. After the gruesome beating, I couldn't move. The only reason she stopped was that the police showed up and restrained her. Bonnie was rushed to the nearest hospital by ambulance. They rushed me to the hospital as well because they thought my mother had killed me.

After the beating incident, the police took my mother to jail. A social worker was called to the hospital to talk to me. She was an old lady by the name of Rebecca Riley. She asked over and over, "Why, Reagus? Why?"

"I had dreamed over and over about eating Bonnie Logan. Today, I couldn't hold back the urge to eat her. She tasted so good, and her skin was so soft."

"How did you begin to like eating people?" she asked again.

"Stop asking me that silly question. I loved it. Now, leave me the hell alone before I turn on you," I screamed, as I exited the door to run, but the police stood outside, stopping me. I kicked and kicked until the doctor sedated me. I was a child, so they kept me in the system for about ten years until

they thought eating people was out of my system. I was released on May 2, 2014.

My mother had gotten out of jail and began using crack heavily. She had moved from Forest, Mississippi because they burned crosses in her yard—as if we were niggas. They burned her house down to the ground too. She met this new boyfriend, John Benton, who was abusive and on drugs too. He would get high and beat my mother until she was unconscious. She continued to be beaten like that because John was supplying her with crack. By this time, they had two twins, a boy, Kyle, and a girl, Kale. My mother was pregnant with them when I was committed to East Central Mental Institute. After I got out, she had a baby girl, Amber Rose.

Arriving home, I stepped into this ragged, three-bedroom apartment with clothes all over the floor and no food in the refrigerator. There were dirty dishes in the sink, the bathtub was filled with brown water, and feces were all over the toilet.

"Your room is in there, killer. Make yourself at home and try not to eat any of my children," Mother remarked with this dirty smirk on her face. She looked so different from the last time I had seen her. As I looked at her, she had cut her silky, blonde hair, her teeth were missing, and she had sores all over her body.

"My name is Reagus, not killer. You have jokes about eating your children. What if they

decided they wanted to eat me?" I remarked back, hoping to get a reaction from her.

"You will be whatever I want you to be. You should want me to call you that since you were sent away for eating a girl's leg. Have you forgotten about that, killer?" she snapped, as she walked up to me and smacked me across the face.

Grabbing her hand, I stared at her, eye to eye. Mother pulled away and rushed into her bedroom. Before closing the door, she looked back at me with a strange look on her face.

Opening the door to my so-called room, it had two dirty white mattresses laid out on the floor with one small, brown, wooden dresser. I walked in and closed the door. Locking the door behind me, I investigated the closet and saw nothing but a big ass rat. It looked like a rabbit running into this big hole deep within the closet. I felt pissed off and very angry. I was so angry that I wanted to go into my mother's room and kill her dead. So many dark and dangerous thoughts ran through my mind at that time. I was better off at the mental institution.

Exiting the room, I walked to the living room, noticing the twins sitting on the couch. Kyle and Kale sat on the couch, staring at me. So, I decided to introduce myself because I knew they didn't have a clue about who I was and why I was there.

*"I'm Reagus. Do you two know who I am?"
I asked, as I looked at them sitting there with the
same features as our mother.*

*"Yes, we do. Mother said you are our
brother that got locked up for eating some girl's
leg," Kale stated, as she stood up and extended her
hand to shake mine.*

"She told you that?"

*"Yes, she did," Kyle stated, as he stood up
as well and extended his hand to be greeted.*

*"We don't care what you did, Reagus. We
are glad you are home with us." Kale smiled, as she
hugged me. I hugged her back, and she had this
terrible smell to her. It was like she hadn't taken a
bath in weeks.*

*"Thank you, Kale," I replied, then Kyle
hugged me. We all stood there in a group hug for at
least two minutes.*

*"What were you two doing?" I asked, as I
pulled back from the group. Their stench was
getting to my nose.*

*"We are sitting here, hungry as usual," Kyle
spoke out. He seemed like the more outspoken of the
two.*

*"Why don't you go in the kitchen and eat?"
I replied.*

*"What do you want us to eat, sandwiches?"
Kale added, as she wiped her face and walked into
the kitchen. Following her to the refrigerator, there*

was a jug of water. There was no sign of food. She bent over, looking farther into the refrigerator, and all I could think about what biting her upper arm. Her arms and legs were so smooth and looked delicious, but she stank.

I began to drool when Kyle interrupted, "Why are you looking at Kale like that?"

"No reason. I'm thinking of how I can get us something to eat. How long has it been since you two have eaten?"

"We haven't eaten since yesterday around noon. You will see it's hard getting a meal around here every day. Anyway, I'm going to the store," Kale interrupted.

"You don't have any money," Kyle pointed out.

"So, Kyle, it's not like we haven't stolen food before. Are you going to the store or not? I'm not standing around here hungry another day. If we go to jail, then we go to jail. At least we will get something to eat in there," Kale replied, as she stared at Kyle.

"Hold on, you two thieves. I will figure out a way to feed us. You two just chill before you end up in jail. Trust me, you don't want to be locked down like an animal," I said, as my memory took me back to the mental institution for a second.

"Why were you locked up?" they both asked at the same time.

"No reason, just mistaken identity," I spoke with laughter.

"Yeah, right. You probably were eating on that girl as they said. How did she taste?" Kyle smirked while having a devilish look on his face.

"If you already know, then why ask me?"

"We just wanted to hear you say you ate that girl," Kyle stated.

"I didn't eat any girl. I bit her leg but didn't eat her. There is a big difference. Anyway, are you two finished asking me questions? Now, you know the truth. I bit a girl, and they sent me away to a mental institution. All that matters is that I'm home now," I explained, hoping they wouldn't keep bringing Bonnie Logan up.

We all walked back into the living room when Mother came out to join us. She walked up to me and handed me fifty dollars. "Go buy some food for the house and don't bring back no snacks. Real food. Those two over there don't know how to do anything right."

"I don't know where to go," I replied, as I took the money from her hand.

"I'll take you to the store, Reagus, since Robin doesn't trust Kale and me to buy food," Kyle interrupted, as he walked past Mother and gave her a slight push with his shoulders. She pushed him in the back, and he stopped in his tracks, just staring back at her.

"I'm going with you two," Kale spoke, as she walked before Kyle and gave him a push toward the door. Before she exited, she grabbed this big purse half her size.

Mother stood there in defense, and that was when I noticed her pretty face. Even though she had sores on her face, my thoughts went to eating her jaws. Licking my lips, I walked out the door with a big smile on my face. Kale and Kyle seemed to know their way around Walnut Grove, Mississippi. My mom moved from Forest when I bit that little girl. She figured people would forget about me long after I had gone away.

We walked to the local grocery store called Piggly Wiggly. I got a cart, and we shopped. As I put food in the cart, Kale put more food in her big purse. My only fear was we were going to get busted. I wasn't looking forward to going to jail, so I tried to stay away from Kale. Only two cashiers were present, and the manager was in this small office.

I began putting the groceries on the roller bed, while the cashier rang them up. Kale stood there like she had done nothing wrong. I glimpsed down at her purse, and it was full. I was hoping the cashier didn't call the police, as she stared at Kale. And of course, Kale stared at her back. After I paid for the food, we all walked out and headed back to the apartment.

She was like a smooth criminal, stealing. I didn't realize that Kyle had food in his pants. They both had stolen food from Piggly Wiggly.

"How long have you two been stealing food? It seems like you two have been doing this a very long time," I asked them, as we walked down the street to the apartment.

"We have been stealing since we were four years old. Robin and John started us stealing, and we decided to do it on our own. Sometimes, we ask the store manager for food, and he gives it to us," Kale answered with a blank look on her face.

"I see. Why do you call them Robin and John and not Mother and Daddy?" I asked.

Kale jumped in. "We're not calling them crackheads Mom and Dad. Are you crazy? You can call them that, but we aren't."

"I'm not doing it either. You haven't been through the stuff we have. They will always be Robin and John. The two don't act like parents," Kyle remarked.

"Well, Robin and John it is," I said.

"Why?" Kyle spoke with attitude.

"I just asked, fool; I'm on your side and don't ever forget that. I know I'm a stranger right now, but I am your brother," I replied.

"Can we trust you?" Kyle asked, as he stopped and looked at me.

"Yes, you can trust me. Did I tell the people at the store you were stealing food? No, I didn't tell them. I'm on your side, and I promise from this day forward, you won't go hungry again."

"You promise we will never go hungry again?" Kale asked, as tears formed in her eyes, staring at me.

"Yes, I promise. And you two won't have to steal again. I am here to take care of you. Forgot about Robin or John. I am here to protect you," I assured them, as I put my arm around Kale, and we continued back.

"Can you help us do something about these clothes too? I'm tired of getting picked on at school," Kyle asked.

"Me too," Kale joined in.

"I will work on getting us help because it doesn't seem like a mother is helping out much."

"Robin is doing her own thing. She is so high sometimes that she doesn't even realize we are not home," Kale said.

"You don't want to at least try to call her Mother?" I asked again.

"No. She doesn't deserve to be called Mother," Kyle said.

I investigated Kyle and Kale's eyes and wondered what all Mother had put them through over the years. They probably had a hard life like me when I was coming up. As we walked home, I saw all kinds of homeless people everywhere. They were begging for food, and one old, Black man tried to take the food we had just gotten. I lost it and beat him half to death. I stopped because Kale was screaming out to me. I had picked up a two by four plank nearby and went to work on him. The rest of the homeless people backed away, fearing me. I didn't realize that I had that much rage inside of me.

****

Dr. Amanda Smith asked, "Who was your first complete meal, and how did you devour him or her?"

"That's an easy answer. My baby sister, Amber Rose, was my very first complete meal. She was useless in the world anyway. It was better for us to eat her than for her to suffer as we did. Kale and Kyle didn't know they were eating her, but who cares? Their stomachs were full. No more hunger pains while going to bed at night for a few days," I answered.

Occurred Incident: FULL MEAL

Time passed, and we moved to Sebastopol, Mississippi. Amber Rose was born on June 16, 2014. She turned two months old on my birthday, August 16. Kale and Kyle were ten years old at the time.

Mother had signed me into a GED program. She changed my name to Reagus Benton. She put white out on my real name and changed all my other paperwork. Until this day, I don't know how she got away with it. To me, a crackhead made no sense and just wanted to get high all the time. Her actions surprised me. Her explanation for being so deceitful was that she didn't want to move again. She tried hard to hide the truth from everyone – the truth of me being a cannibal.

I didn't know that people thought I had died in the mental institution after I had bitten Bonnie Logan. They all thought the KKK clan had killed me. Until this day, I don't know why the KKK was involved. As you can see, I am biracial. They wanted to hang me and make me suffer for my crime. Later, after I was put away, I learned her father was a member of the KKK. That was probably why they wanted me to die a harsh death.

My mother had told everyone I died. So, when I appeared back on the scene, she told everyone that I was someone on the streets she had taken in. Those people were so gullible and dense. Why would an unfit mother take a teenager off the streets, and she couldn't take care of herself?

Moving on to my first human meal. I came home, and my mother was getting food out of the refrigerator and packing it into bags. She had done it before, but this time, I busted her. She looked at me like a deer caught in headlights.

"What are you doing?" I yelled, hoping she would stop stealing our food and leave.

"None of your business, killer," she angrily replied, as she continued to keep putting food into bags.

"Why are you taking food from us? We don't have any more money. We will starve to death."

"You kids won't starve, just get out and beg. You can get some more food. John's mother needs something to eat," she explained, probably hoping I would let it go.

"I don't care about John's mama. Your kids come first. I'm bringing food into this house and feeding these hungry kids. I'm tired of taking care of your responsibility," I yelled.

"Who cares, killer? You can give them just one meal."

"One meal. You are taking everything. I can't let you leave us hungry like this. Put it back," I yelled, as I got in her face.

"You little bastard, I'm your mother. I will tell you what to do. I'm taking this food and leaving."

"Put it back," I yelled again, pushing her to the floor. Mother jumped up and shoved me back. I snatched the bag of food off the floor, and she grabbed it.

"No, Reagus, I'm taking this bag."

"This is all the food we have, but if you prefer your children to starve, then take it. Once you leave, then we will disown you. You'll be a stranger to us. Anytime a mother takes food from her children to feed her boyfriend and his mother is sad," I stated with a serious look on my face. I saw myself killing her that day, but I let her live.

"This is my house, boy. Watch your mouth. Don't you forget I raised you!"

"You mean the mental institution raised me. I'm a killer, as you say. So, get out before I kill you," I threatened, taking a step toward her with my hands relaxed by my side.

"Don't you dare touch me, boy," Robin replied, as she walked out the door with the bag in her hand. I had gotten so tired of her stealing food and other things from us. I wanted to kill her then, but I restrained myself. As I turned around to go back into the kitchen to see what she had gotten, I heard the baby crying in the bedroom. Walking to the back, Amber lay out on a filthy, stinking mattress. The room reeked of weed and alcohol.

Picking up Amber Rose, I stared at her ugly face for a few minutes until she drooled on my hand. My mind wanted me to toss her across the room for drooling on me, but the hairs on the back of my neck began to stand tall. My tongue hung from my mouth and slob lingered, dripping onto my shirt. Wiping my mouth and cradling her in my arms like a baby should be, I began sniffing her. Her smell reminded me so much of Bonnie Logan. At that moment, I knew she had to be eaten. Today was her day to die.

As I walked back into the kitchen, holding Amber Rose, she cried, as I fixed her a bottle of milk. I poured a full bottle of Benadryl into the bottle as well. Feeding Amber Rose made my stomach growl. At first, I felt light-headed at the thought of eating my baby sister. But that feeling quickly faded.

After I fed her, I gave her a warm bath, hoping it would help put her to sleep fast. Amber Rose indeed fell asleep before I finished her bath. I sniffed her every chance I got. Her sweet smell had mesmerized me. I couldn't take it anymore; I had to taste her. Releasing her sleeping body in the water, I proceeded to my mother's room and got John's hunter's knife. Staring at the knife, I undressed myself down to my underwear because I knew it would be a mess. I should have just eaten her right there. Entering the bathroom, I began tearing off her meat, piece by piece, because I knew the others were going to be hungry later.

I didn't know if she was dead or not from all the Benadryl I gave her, but I knew she never woke up. Before I carved her to pieces, I dried her off and began eating right there. Ripping off piece after piece, I was in Heaven. This was the first time I could enjoy eating what I had been craving for years. After pleasing myself with delicious bites, I began to carve her feet off and tossed them into the garbage bag. Then, I cut off her small hands and decapitated her head from her body, tossing them into the garbage bag. Carving her body to pieces in the bathtub, so I would not get blood everywhere, I continued to eat more of her than I'd placed in the garbage bag. Finally, I sliced her into many pieces, so I could roast her.

After the carving of Amber Rose, I put her mutilated body in a big roasting pan that I found outside in the dumpster. I checked for holes before I began my roast. Running to my bedroom, I took out a bag of Irish potatoes I had hidden in the closet from Mother. Slicing ten potatoes with a whole onion and bell peppers, I seasoned the pieces with Lawry seasoned sauce and Worcestershire sauce. It was time for my dish.

Putting Pam cooking spray around the pan to make sure it didn't stick, like you would regular meat, I placed the mutilated baby inside. Placing the lid over the food, I turned the stove on to four hundred degrees. As Amber Rose cooked, I placed the other parts into almost eight garbage bags. After putting on more clothes, I left the apartment with a big bag of garbage and a bleach bottle. Walking to the back of the apartment complex to the dumpster, I saw two little kids playing, so I had to run them off. They cursed me like they were grown, and I promised to beat their tails if I saw them again. At the dumpster, I opened the garbage bag and poured the whole bottle of bleach into it. The bleach leaked out, but I poured it until it was empty. Tying the bag up, I threw the bag of garbage away with the empty bleach bottle.

Looking around to see if anyone was looking, I dusted my pants off and rushed back to the apartment. As I opened the door, the next-door neighbor's daughter, Joyce Myers, came out of her apartment carrying a big chocolate sheet cake with white candles.

"Happy birthday, Reagus," she yelled out. My mouth fell open with surprise. I didn't know whether to run or embrace her. She continued, "Well, are you going to say something or not?"

"I'm sorry. You just took me by surprise," I replied with my mouth still open.

"Here you go. I baked this chocolate cake especially for you."

"Thank you, Joyce. No one has ever given me anything for my birthday."

"You're welcome. I like you and want to do something special for you."

"Again, thank you."

"Well, are you going to invite me in or not?" Joyce insisted.

"I would, but my mother will be home soon, and I don't want to hear her mouth. She has already threatened to beat me today, and she doesn't need any more drama. But maybe next time," I replied, as I tried to walk away.

"Okay. I will be looking forward to seeing you soon. If you know what I mean."

"Sure," I replied, as I took the cake and went inside the apartment. My heart was about to jump out of my chest, as I relaxed on the door, looking down at the cake. A big smile came over me. I was having my favorite food and my favorite cake on my birthday. I felt very lucky.

Placing the cake on the table, I immediately began cleaning up the entire house with bleach, getting rid of any blood that lingered around.

After I finished baking Amber Rose, I just had to taste a piece before Kyle and Kale got there. OMG... she tasted so good. Better than Bonnie Logan. Before I could eat another piece, Kyle and Kale rushed through the door with their eyes open wide.

"Something smells so good," Kale called out, as she made her way to the kitchen.

"I'm ready to eat. What are we having?" Kyle asked, as he tossed his bookbag on the floor, heading into the kitchen.

"We are having roast and cake. I need some rice and gravy. Can y'all wait?"

"I don't want no rice. I'm hungry now,"
Kyle yelled out while sitting at the kitchen table.

"Why don't you two start on your homework, and I will prepare some rice? I bought some rice in a bag, so it will take about ten minutes. And it won't take long for the gravy," I stated, as I began to prepare the rice and gravy.

"Homework. I don't have any," Kyle smarted off.

"Yeah, right. Do your work and I will let you eat until you can't eat no more," I stated.

Kyle's eyes lit up like a Christmas tree. He was ready to chow down. As they did homework in the living room, I finished preparing the rice and gravy. Kyle kept looking into the kitchen like he was starving to death. Truth was, he might be starving. If he only knew.

After I finished everything, we all sat down for the first time as a family and began to eat. I put the rice on the table while placing chunks of meat and gravy over it. We all sat there and ate Amber Rose. I moaned every time I took a bite. The meat was so delicious.

"Where's Amber Rose?" Kale asked.

"Robin took her when she came by here stealing our food out of the refrigerator," I responded without looking at her.

"Not again," Kyle replied, as he jumped up and opened the refrigerator. He continued, "We

work so hard to keep food in here."

"I know, Kyle. We had a long talk. I don't think she will do it again."

"I hope not because I'm getting tired of this," he replied while sitting back down to finish eating.

"Why does it smell like bleach in here?" Kale asked, as she chewed her meat.

"I cleaned up before I cooked. There was an awful smell in here."

"Oh, okay," she said, as she continued to eat up her food in a rush.

That day we ate and ate until our bellies couldn't take anymore. I cleaned the entire apartment with bleach that night, as they slept. I cleaned up like I was a maid. I was so happy and very excited about my birthday. We ate Amber Rose for about three days until it was all gone. I ate the best meat ever, and I wasn't going to stop there. This was only the beginning of tasting my favorite meat: human flesh.

CHAPTER 3

(Separation Issues)

Dr. Amanda Smith asked, "I noticed that you haven't mentioned your father. How did you feel not having him in your life?"

"I didn't feel anything after the day that coward bastard left me standing in my grandparents' yard, crying and screaming for him to not leave me. A child should never have to experience being abandoned by a parent who is supposed to have unconditional love for them. A parent is supposed to protect their child from harm. I suffered after my father deserted me. After not seeing him for months, I became numb and very angry. My violence level was beyond control. The first week I was put into the East Mississippi Mental Institution, the people feared me. Their fear is what kept me alive in there," I answered, as I put my head down.

Occurred Incident: ABSENT FATHER
First Meeting: Age five
"Please don't leave me," I begged my father, even though this was our first time meeting at the tender age of five.

"I don't know you. I just heard that Robin was saying she had a child, and it was mine. You

could be anyone's child for all I know," he nonchalantly stated.

"You are my father. She told me."

"No, I'm not. I wish you and your gold-digging mother would leave me alone and leave my parents alone. All your mother wants is money, and I'm not going to give her a dime," he stated again.

"She doesn't want no money," I replied, as I looked at my mother, and she looked away. I continued, "Tell him, Mother, that you don't want money."

"Well, that's not exactly true, Reagus. We need money to eat," Mother spoke out, as she looked at Father with an evil look.

"See, I told you. I'm not giving y'all anything. You know this boy ain't my child. He looks nothing like me," my father stated, as he flicked a piece of my blonde hair.

"You're crazy, Raymond. You know you were the only one I had been with at that time, so don't try to act like I was out sleeping with everyone," Mother replied, as they stood toe to toe, staring at each other.

I grabbed my father's hand and began to cry. He snatched his hand away quickly. I took a deep sniff before he did. His skin smelled so good, maybe kind of like a rosy smell. It smelled so good that I wanted to lick his hand. Maybe even take a bite out of it.

"Don't try to throw this child on me, Robin, and get away from my parents' house. If I hear you're getting money from them, I will kill you," Father threatened.

"Go ahead and kill me now. You're going straight to jail."

"That's what you want, but that's not happening. All I must do is..." His voice trailed off, as he looked toward me when I grabbed his arm again, holding tight. "Young man, I know you desperately want to know who your father is, but I'm not it. I know your mother has told you this, but I am not him," he explained, much calmer now.

"Stop telling him lies, Raymond. You know that you're his father. Give me a blood test and you will see. You don't want to accept the responsibility, but I will make you pay me. I won't let you get away with this," Robin threatened, as she grabbed me. She tried pulling me away, but I held on to my father like it was the last time I was going to see him.

"Let him go, Reagus. He is going to pay for this," Robin spoke, as she snatched me away, and we headed out the door. Father was right on our heels.

"You need to find that child the right father and keep my name out of your mouth. Stop coming around here, trying to make my mom and dad feel guilty about a child that ain't mine. Something told *me to come by here, and here you are, hustling my parents again."*

"I'm not hustling anybody. Those are Reagus' grandparents, whether you like it or not. But you don't have to worry about that. He will never come around here again," she harshly spoke.

"Good. Get on out of here," he yelled.

"Father, no, don't let her take me away from you. I can't go without you. Please don't go," I begged, as I tried to tear away from her tight grip.

"Get on out of here, boy. And you can stop calling me your father. Tell your boy I'm not his father," he demanded.

"Get in the car, Reagus," Mother yelled.

I broke away from her, running back to my father. I put my arms around him and held on for dear life. I was crying and screaming, not wanting him to go, so he grabbed both of my arms away from around his body and shoved me onto the ground. I fell so hard that I hit my head. Robin just stood by and watched.

As I lay on the ground, crying for my father, he looked down at me and spit. "You'll never be my son."

I placed my hand on his leg. "Please, Father, I love you."

"I don't love you, boy. Never have, never will," he spoke, as he kicked my hand off his leg and walked away.

I reached out to him, but he never looked back. Suddenly, Robin snatched me up by the collar of my shirt.

"Come on, boy. I can't believe we didn't get no damn money," she voiced madly, as she opened the car door and threw me in.

I cried as we pulled away. I could still see my father walking away without looking back. Robin pulled off quickly. I kept looking back until he disappeared. I cried all the way home. All I could think about was why my father didn't want me.

Meeting: Age 15

At the age of fifteen, I was locked down at East Mississippi Mental Institution. They considered me violent. Whenever a visitor came, I was locked in handcuffs, and a doctor had to be on standby. Sometimes, I had to wear a face mask because I had bitten so many people. That smell was overpowering me, and I couldn't help myself at times. But today, my father came to visit me. He looked the same besides a few gray hairs embedded in his mustache and beard.

"Can you please take this mask off him, so he can talk? Y'all have him locked up like an animal," Father asked.

"We don't think it will be safe," Dr. Steven Smith stated.

"Well, I need him to be able to talk about it if you don't mind. I don't think he will harm his father."

"Maybe he will. I didn't want you to visit because you are the reason for most of his violent spells. Maybe this was a bad idea," Dr. Steven Smith stated, as he stood up and grabbed me by the arm. I snatched away and began staring at my father. I wanted to hear what this cold-hearted bastard had to say.

"See, he doesn't want to go. Now, remove the mask because I think he wants to respond to what I have to say," Father spoke with a smirk on his face.

A male nurse walked over after Dr. Steven Smith motioned him to. He began taking off the mask. He had this distraught look on his face, as he stared at my father. He was scared. I noticed his hands trembling a little. Father looked at the guy's hands and then at his face.

"What do you want?" I harshly spoke as soon as the mask released my face.

"I know you're shocked to see me, but..." He stopped in mid-sentence.

"What is it?" I spoke again. Dr. Steven Smith shifted in his seat, as he stared at me, and my stare was directly at my father. He could tell that I was about to strike, but I remained calm.

"Well, damn, boy, give me time to talk. We finally got blood tests done, and it looks like I am your daddy," he explained.

"So? I don't care if you are or not. You destroyed that years ago."

"I know I did, and hopefully, one day you will forgive me," he replied. Something was telling me that this man wasn't sincere. He had a motive.

"Why are you here lying? What is the real reason you are here? I haven't seen your ugly ass face until now. What do you want?" I asked again.

"Well, I'm about to do this television interview, and I needed a little more information about you." He told the truth.

"So, that's why you have shown up here. What interview?" I asked.

"We should go, Reagus. Mr. Dune, that's not the conversation we talked about. I told you that information like that would trigger violence," Dr. Steven Smith explained, as he stood to his feet.

"He ain't violent. He is calm. We are having a father/son talk. So, please sit down and let me finish," Father stated, as he stared back at me. He continued, *"They wanted to know about you eating on that little girl."*

"Mr. Dune," Dr. Steven Smith called out.

"Wait, Dr. Smith. I have an answer," I replied calmly.

"You don't have to answer him, Reagus. This visit is over," Dr. Steven Smith said, as he motioned for the male nurse to walk back over.

"No, it's not over. I said I wanted to answer the question. Now, sit down and let me talk," I spoke with a little harshness. The male nurse began walking over but dropped the mask. I paused for a few seconds and gave him a serious look.

"Nurse Taylor, please get someone to clean the mask off immediately," Dr. Steven Smith quickly stated. He knew how I felt about a dirty mask. Nothing pissed me off more than being dirty.

"Yes, sir," he quickly replied, as he switched out with another nurse to clean up the mask. The second male nurse that entered the room was a Black man whom I liked. He was kind and very respectful.

"Finish," I spoke to Father.

"Can I ask you a few questions?" he asked, as he pulled out a piece of paper and pen.

"You mean to tell me that you didn't come here to bond with me, but you came here to get answers for a TV interview. Why does she want to interview you and not Robin?" I asked.

"Robin is on crack bad," he responded.

"Mr. Dune." Dr. Steven Smith interrupted.

"Well, it's the truth. She is strung out bad, and they thought it would be better for me to talk

about the incident of you eating on that girl," he spoke.

"That sucks. I thought you wanted to love me."

"Boy, stop. I don't love you. Like I said before, never have and never will. Right now, I just need answers on why you tried to eat that girl," he stated with a serious look on his face.

"I guess it's about money."

"Answer the question. Everybody keeps telling me how sick you are, in here biting chunks out of people and shit. You must be sick or something. Your mama didn't tell me all that, but I am beginning to believe it, just how sick are you," Father snapped.

"You dirty piece of shit. You're just like Robin. Neither one of you wanted me. I was probably a one-night stand."

"Well, Robin wanted to get high, and I wanted sex, even trade, but it resulted in you. I wasn't ready for a child. Children make me sick. I rather fuck them and send them on their way with busted, bleeding assholes," he stated with no smile.

"You're a pedophile."

"Call me what you want. Robin knew to take you away. If you had stayed with me, I would have made you my little bitch," he choked up.

"Mr. Dune," Dr. Steven Smith yelled. I stood immediately but didn't react. They had that straitjacket on tight.

"You don't have to keep calling my name. I'm ready to get out of here anyway. I don't want to see this freak anymore. I should have taken him in and fucked him every day." Father laughed, as he stared me down.

"I was just a child."

"What's your point?" He smirked, as the nurses rushed him out of my sight.

After the door closed behind him, I sat back down in my chair and just stared at the spot where he once sat. Dr. Smith didn't say a word; he sat back down next to me. I put my head down on the table and cried like a baby.

Third Meeting: Age Twenty

Planting one of my special trees by the black gate, a car pulled up. Stepping out was my father. We stared at each other for a few seconds before he yelled, "Are you going to let me in or what?"

"What do you want?"

"I want to come in and talk."

"I don't have no conversation for you, Raymond Dune. The last time I talked to you, you were talking about having sex with me when I was a child. Now, that's sick," I remarked.

"Well, that makes us even," he replied, as he walked up to the gate.

I walked to the gate and unlocked it. He walked in and walked right past me. Closing the gate but not securing it, I walked behind him.

"What do you want now, Raymond? More information for a television interview?" I asked, as I watched his tiny body walk toward the house. He looked like he was on drugs now, so skinny and fragile.

"You're a gardener now. Last time I saw you, you were locked down like an animal," he stated.

"Well, Raymond, the last time I saw you, you were a big man with big muscles, and now you look like a crackhead," I snapped back.

"Crack does the body well," he replied, as he stopped in his tracks to stare back at me.

"That confirms you're a crackhead, just like Robin. I don't have any money for you, so now you can leave."

"You're so quick to throw me away."

"Just like you have done me all my life."

"That's in the past."

"Maybe to you but not to me. I remember it like it was yesterday," I snapped back, hoping he would just leave.

"Your memory probably sucks from all that medication they pumped in you while you were

locked up," he stated, as he started back walking again, heading around to the back of the house.

"What are you looking for anyway?"

"I know Mama and Daddy had some tools laying around here. I need some of them to fix up stuff," he lied.

"You mean you want the tools to pawn, so you can get yourself a high," I smarted off.

"Yeah, that too. Where are they located? Must be out in the barn," Father said, as he directed his attention toward the barn, as I jumped in front of him.

"You're not just going to take anything from here. If I want you to have them, then I will give them to you, but you're not taking them," I said, as I gave him a little push.

"Don't touch me. Don't ever put your hands on me," he spoke, as he pushed me back.

"Come on, man. Get these tools and get off my property," I stated, as I turned and began walking toward the barn.

"About time you come to your senses. Those are my daddy's tools," he stated, as we entered the barn.

Stopping at the door, I let him walk on into the barn. He was walking along, picking out everything. Within a few minutes, his arms were full. I walked on in behind him. "Is that everything you want?"

"There is plenty more that I need, but I will be back for those."

"No, you won't, Raymond Dune. This will be your last time on my property. I don't want you coming back here," I demanded.

"This is my mama and daddy's property. I can do what I damn well please."

"Not this time, Raymond."

"Watch and see. Maybe next time, I will give you a good fucking in your ass too. Seems like you might like that being locked down in that mental institution, you crazy fuck," Raymond stated.

Suddenly, I picked up the axe laying on the ground and chopped him in his knee from behind. Raymone fell to the ground, grabbing his leg. I swung the axe again, chopping at the same leg and severing it from his body. Raymond screamed, "What the fuck are you doing?"

"Something I should have done years ago."

I chopped the other leg. This time, it separated from his body in one chop.

"Well, Raymond, let's just say you won't be walking out of anybody else's life."

"You're going to pay for this shit," he yelled, as he crawled for the barn door. He screamed at the door.

"Wait, Raymond, you forgot your legs," I taunted, as I picked up both legs and placed them on the table. Picking up some rope, I ran over and

*put it around his neck. Tying a good knot, I began
dragging him toward the woods.*

*"Please don't kill me, you sick fuck,"
Raymond begged, as I choked him.*

*"I'm not going to kill you. You're going to
kill yourself."*

"Just let me go," he managed to get out.

*"Hell no. I'm going to watch you suffer.
This is payback from all those years of pain you
caused me," I replied, as I found a big tree and tied
him to it. Raymond began coughing out of control.*

*I paused for a second until he stopped.
Tying him to the tree, I kicked dirt on him and
walked off.*

*"You can't leave me here bleeding to
death."*

"Watch me."

*"Reagus, don't do this. You're going to kill
me."*

*"No, Raymond, you're going to kill
yourself." I walked off.*

*"I love you, Reagus," he yelled out, and I
stopped in my tracks.*

*"I love you," he repeated. A tear escaped
my eye, but I kept walking without looking back. He
screamed and screamed, but I didn't care.*

*After a week passed by, I walked through the
woods to see if Raymond was dead. I was sure he
was but had to see. As I walked up toward the tree, I*

noticed that pieces of his body were there. Something had eaten him. Looking around the woods, I smiled and walked back toward the house. That was one of the happiest moments of my life to know that a deadbeat dad like him was dead.

****

Dr. Amanda Smith asked, "How did you feel when your mother separated you from your siblings?"

"At first, I was happy because I didn't have to take care of them anymore. But deep down, I missed them like crazy, especially when it was time to eat our favorite meat," I responded.

Occurred Incident: Separation

I was so glad today was the last day of school before Christmas break. I bought the twins a new game and clothes. Working hard every day, I bought so many different things for the house. I even invested in a new house phone. All my gifts were at the shelter because I didn't want Kyle and Kale to find them. They would open them and then try to rewrap the gifts. So, I couldn't take any chances.

Arriving at the job, I decided to go to Mary Alice's office and call home. As soon as someone picked up the phone that I didn't recognize, my mouth fell open.

"Who is this?" I snapped, as I stared at the phone, hoping it was Robin.

"Boy, don't you recognize your mama?" Mother replied.

"What are you doing there? I thought I told you to leave and never return."

"Remember, you little sick bastard, this is my house. And where in the hell did you get all this meat?" she replied. It seemed like she was chewing.

"Get out of my house. Where are Kyle and Kale?" I asked.

"Boy, they are here with a few more kids, eating barbeque."

"What barbeque? I hadn't cooked no barbeque for them," I said, hoping they weren't eating my favorite meat, but something told me they were.

"Well, John decided to barbecue some of that meat. I cooked baked beans, potato salad, and...."

Before she could continue, I yelled, "Get the hell out of my house."

"You can just come home, boy, and pack your things because once you get here, there are going to be some new rules around here. John and I are moving back home. And you are moving out," she stated, as she hung up the phone in my face.

All that evening at work, I couldn't help but think about what she had said to me. She had been missing for months and now expected to come back acting like a mother. That heifer needed to get real. As soon as ten o'clock rolled around, I ran all the way home. I walked up to the apartment and saw John outside, still barbequing my meat. It seemed like the whole neighborhood was there. They didn't have any idea what they were eating.

"What's up, boy?" John yelled out with a Budweiser in his hand.

"Where's Robin?" I asked.

"Her nasty ass is in the house. What? You're not happy to see us come home?"

I didn't say anything else to him but walked off. He gave me this weird look. Before I walked into the apartment, we stood there, staring at each other eye to eye for a few seconds. Walking inside the apartment, Mother was in the kitchen with Kyle and Kale.

"Why are all these people inside our house?" I snapped, looking at the two. We had agreed that they were not going to invite Mother in without my permission.

"You're so stupid. This is my house. And these are my kids, not yours," she stated.

"You left your house months ago. And remember, you abandoned your kids for your boyfriend."

"It doesn't matter; you can get your clothes and go. I came back to let you know that your grandparents are dead. Your deadbeat daddy tracked me down to let me know. They have a will, and all the money is left for you. You need to go get our money." She laughed, as she continued to eat the meat.

"How long have they been dead? Where are they located?"

"They have been dead for about two months now. I decided to come and tell you before I forget again."

"Yeah, that's what crack will do to you. You must love that stuff because you killed your baby, and then you left your kids to take care of themselves. Damn, you do deserve the mother of the year award." I smirked, as I stood back, waiting for her to attack me like always.

"Get your clothes and get out of my house. And don't you ever come back here unless you bring back that money, or I will tell the cops what happened to Amber Rose," she threatened.

"What happened, Mother? You killed your baby?" I remarked.

"It doesn't matter, killer. Get out now," she politely spoke.

"I'm going to get out, Robin, but don't you ever expect to see any of that money. I'm not giving

you a dime. You kept me from them, and now, you want their money."

Kyle interrupted, "I'm going with Reagus."

"Me too," Kale spoke up.

"You two kids are not going anywhere. Let this killer live by himself. He deserves to be by himself."

I didn't say another word to Robin or the twins. Packing all my clothes into bags, I left the apartment and never returned. In a way, those kids were like a monkey off my back. I was finally relieved.

I walked back to the shelter with all my clothes. Mary Alice was still up. I let her know what happened between me and Robin. She consoled me and gave me one of the rooms in the shelter until the next morning.

The next day, Mary Alice drove me out to my grandparents' farm. We went down this street called Patrick Drive. Driving down to this old brick house on the left, we turned onto this dirt road. There were many houses and trailers around, but my grandparents' estate was in the back. Mary Alice drove deeper down this dirt road until we came to a sign that said Jersey Joe Patrick Estates. There was a black gate blocking the driveway. I got out, and the chain wasn't locked, so I opened the gate. We drove down this scary dirt road to a large brick house. It had an old brown barn and then another building where they slaughtered hogs.

As we pulled up to this grayish brick house with green shutters, a lanky man stepped out the door. Mary Alice and I looked at each other and stepped out of the van.

"Can I help y'all?" he asked.

"Yes, sir. I'm here because they said my grandparents died. I came to see if it was true," I said.

"Who are you, boy?"

"I'm Reagus Dune. My mother is Robin Dune."

"Reagus Dune, Robin's boy is dead."

"No, sir, I'm not dead. She's the one who told me about my grandparents. Why would you think I'm dead?" I asked as if I didn't already know the answer. They all thought I was killed by the KKK clan. Robin had run the whole story down to me one day when she came to visit me in East Central.

"Damn, boy, you still biting folks and shit. Where have you been?"

"It doesn't matter; who are you?"

"I'm your Uncle Earl; I've been taking care of my parents until they died. We were all shocked when we found out they left you all their money and property. Since we thought you were dead, the money is on hold at the lawyer's office."

"What lawyer?"

"Attorney Jimmy Jones. His office is down by the Sonic's building," he spoke.

After the small talk, Uncle Earl took me around the property, showing me everything. We walked through this big, brick house, and he let me pick out my room. Of course, I took the master bedroom. Nobody lived in the house; he was there probably trying to find out how much he could sell.

We walked around the barn, and there were no animals. It was kind of stupid to me to have a barn and no animals. After that, we walked over to the slaughterhouse. Blood was all over the place.

"Is that blood?" I asked.

"Yeah, boy, it's hog blood. We all slaughter our hogs here on the property. Is that going to be a problem for you?" he replied.

"I don't know; it might be. Who all use this slaughterhouse?"

"All your family. We all have parties up here sometimes," he explained.

"Okay. Well, since I'm here, you all will need to ask me before you come up here. This is my house now, and I don't like for my privacy to be invaded."

Uncle Earl looked at me like I was nothing. I guess he was saying that I was a child, and I didn't tell him or the rest of them what to do. I guess I would have to buy a gun to keep all these people away. I had plans for this slaughterhouse, and it wasn't slicing hogs either. I could see my favorite meal laid out everywhere. I got so excited that I began to laugh out loud. Uncle Earl looked at me and walked off. He probably thought I was crazy as fuck.

I moved my three bags into the master bedroom and asked Mary Alice to take me to the lawyer's office. I arrived and talked to Attorney Jimmy Jones. He prepared the paperwork for me to sign and handed me a check for five hundred thousand dollars. My heart fell deep into my pants. I opened a bank account at The Citizens Bank.

After we left the attorney's office, Mary Alice took me to the shelter. I wanted to stay there for a few days because of my job. I didn't have a car to drive home. My grandparents' house was fifteen minutes outside of town.

The next day, I asked Mary Alice to take me back to the house, and as we pulled up at the gate, people from Scott County Times were there wanting to know if I was the Reagus Dune who people thought was dead. Everyone wanted to talk to the little kid who bit the plugs out of a nine-year-old girl's leg. I figured that people had forgotten about that, but I guess they didn't have any more news to spread.

Years went by, and I had people appear from time to time at my door, asking if I was the

Reagus Dune. At first, I liked the attention, then it began to bother me because I couldn't gather my favorite meat. I was getting hungrier. I was like a vampire ready to strike.

CHAPTER 4

(Extreme Urges)

Dr. Amanda Smith asked, "Did you ever try to fight the urge and craving to eat humans?"

"I have never thought about fighting the urge because I planned out how I was going to kill and eat more of my favorite meat. After eating Amber Rose, I couldn't fight the urge. It was time to eat again," I answered back.

Occurred Incident: THE URGE

I had finally gotten a full-time job at this homeless shelter down the street from the apartment. The rent was based on Robin's income, so we only had to pay $11.00 plus electricity and cable. I bought food and name-brand clothes for Kyle and Kale. Plus, I shopped at the Goodwill store for clothes too.

It was almost Thanksgiving, and I wanted to taste more of my favorite meat. Kyle and Kale put in a request for a roast like we had on my birthday. They were beginning to crave it too. When they got older, I would let them in on my secret. Truth be told, as they got older, they would begin to crave more and more human meat.

While working at the shelter on Thanksgiving, a family I didn't recognize came in. It was an older woman and two little boys. Standing in line, issuing food, one of the little boys ran around the table and began to hug me. I stopped serving and picked him up, giving him a huge hug. His smell was freaking unbearable. Giving him another squeeze, I had to put him down before I sank my teeth right into his big jaws. It took everything in my power to stop me from biting a chunk out of his face. After putting him down, he smiled at me then ran back to his mother. She looked at me, and I gave her the biggest, most trusting smile you ever wanted to see. It was something about her facial features that caught my attention. She seemed sad. I decided at that moment that I was going to befriend her so that I could eat her son. He was going to die by my hands.

The little boy kept staring at me. He would come over and give me a huge hug. It seemed like he wanted me to eat him. The more I put my arms around him, the more I craved eating him. He is the perfect Christmas dinner meal, I thought. Kyle and Kale wanted roast, so I was going to give them roast. After everyone sat down and ate, I prepared my plan to take the little boy and kill him. His mother had planned to stay at the shelter tonight. That was my only opportunity to take him away. I craved him so much that I began to start shaking like a leaf on a tree. There was no way I could leave the homeless shelter without him.

Around three o'clock in the morning, I prepared to go back to the shelter. Peeping in on Kale and Kyle, they were out cold. I'd put a little Benadryl in their Kool-Aid to help them sleep, while I kidnapped this kid. I knew they sometimes sneaked out at night, so that night, I had to make sure they slept without interruption. I didn't want to take a chance of getting caught.

As soon as I stepped outside, Joyce was sitting on the stairs, looking out into the woods. I couldn't rush back in because she had seen me. So, I walked out.

"Hi, Reagus. What are you doing up so late?" she asked.

"I should be asking you the same things. Do you know what time it is?"

"Yes, I do. I wanted to get some fresh air."

"Sure. Do you think I'm stupid? Whom are you waiting on?" I asked.

"To be honest, I was hoping you came outside. I haven't seen you lately. Where have you been?" she asked, changing it around on me.

"I've been working at the homeless shelter up the street to help support me, Kale, and Kyle. You know my mother hasn't been around lately, so someone had to do it," I explained, hoping this conversation would end quickly.

"That's right. I heard my mom say she has run off and left you kids alone."

"Yes, she did, so it's up to me to do everything now."

"I'm so proud of you, Reagus. You go to college; you work to support your family. You are a good kid," she complimented me.

"Kid? I'm a man. Men take care of their families," I replied, as I thought about why I was leaving the house.

"Do you want to come inside my apartment?" she asked.

"No, I have something else to do."

"You are screwing somebody around here?" Joyce asked.

"No."

"Then please come inside. I have something I want to show you," she replied, as she got off the stairs, took me by the hand, and led me inside.

I stopped at the door. "Where are your parents?"

"You know they both work at night."

"That's right. They do."

We stepped inside the apartment, and it smelled like cinnamon. Joyce locked the door behind us and took me to her bedroom. I sat down on the bed, knowing this girl wanted to have sex. My mind was on eating that little boy. I could taste him. As I gathered my thoughts back to Joyce, she stood in front of me, naked. My mind was so focused on eating that kid that I didn't see her get undressed. Looking at her naked, I noticed her flesh looked so clean and very delightful. My log began to rise. I usually took care of myself almost every night by watching porn, but I never felt a real woman.

Joyce got on her knees and unzipped my pants. She exposed me. Her eyes pierced my engorged log like she wanted to eat me. She placed both her hands on me and began swallowing me. My head fell back, and within minutes, I exploded into her mouth. I tried to pull her head back, but she continued until the last drop. I stood up and was about to pull up my pants when she grabbed my private again and continued to suck and suck until I fully erupted again. This time, I began to fondle her big breasts. Looking down at her breasts had me throbbing. All I could think about was slicing off her breasts and putting them on a platter.

I grabbed her by the shoulder and snatched her up. She looked scared at first. Pushing her down on the bed, I found myself tasting her delicious candy. I slid my fingers inside, and it told me she wasn't a virgin. I rose and just admired her body – so smooth and clean. I was ready to eat her entire body. As she caressed me with her hands, I began thinking about eating the flesh of that little boy back at the shelter. I got so excited and hard that I almost released again. This was my first time having sex, but Joyce didn't know that. Focusing on her, I mounted her and gently entered her. We began moving faster, harder, and harder against each other. I was having sex with a real girl. I got so excited that I began doing things that I had seen in this porn scene. Even with all this going on, my mind went back to eating Amber Rose and how good she tasted. Then, I went to think about the little boy at the shelter.

I almost got out of control with Joyce. I flipped her over onto her stomach and pushed deeper into her wound. Joyce was pushing back harder. We had sex for almost an hour until I pulled out, and she devoured me with her mouth. She was very happy when I exited her apartment.

Stepping outside of her apartment, I realized that I had spent too much time over there, and the sun was rising. Walking away from the building, I could see people walking around. That was disappointing for me because there was no way that I could get that little boy to the house without someone seeing him. Kale and Kyle had to be up at 6:30 to go to school. I was very angry.

Early that day, we all headed out to school. Kyle and Kale caught the bus, while Joyce and I walked to Vowell's Market to catch the bus to East Central Community College. They had a bus running Monday through Friday for the ones that didn't have a car. All day at school, my mind was on how good that little boy was going to taste. After the bus dropped us off, I wanted to make a detour to the shelter to see if the little boy was still there, but I couldn't because Joyce was following me like a hound in heat.

After finally getting rid of Joyce, I rushed over to the shelter. To my surprise, the little boy was still there. Mary Alice, the director of the shelter, was watching them because their mother claimed to be gone out looking for a job.

"Hi, Mary Alice. What are you doing with those kids?" I asked, being nosey.

"Do you know that their mother hasn't been here all day? She asked me to watch the little boys and disappeared. I want to call the police, but I'm going to give her a little more time," she explained with a disappointed look on her face.

"I can watch them until I get ready to leave," I insisted, hoping she would open the door I needed to kidnap the one little boy.

"You are so kind. Are you sure you don't mind watching them?"

"I don't mind; I look after my twin brother and sister every day. It will be no problem because I'm here all day after school anyway. Plus, I'm sure these precious little boys will be no problem."

"Okay, Reagus. This tiny one here is called Mike, and this little butterball is called Michael," she explained.

"Great," I happily spoke, as I walked off from her.

Walking over, I introduced myself to the little boys. We began to get along immediately. I played and played with them until it was time to eat. The Michael kid smelled so good, and his flesh tasted delicious. I licked his arm by accident and almost fainted. My eyes rolled in the back of my head, and I immediately became lightheaded. I sniffed the little boy, Mike, and he didn't have the same smell as his brother, Michael. But either way, I had to have them both. I planned to feed little Mike to Kale and Kyle, while I saved Michael all for myself. I pretended to bite him a couple of times when we played, and he did it back to me. If only he knew that he was going to be devoured later that night.

That night around ten o'clock, their mother, Jamie, showed up at the shelter, high as a kite. She was zoned out. I knew she was high because my mother acted the same way. Her lips were dry and white looking. She was scratching as if she had fleas. She came into the room and told me to get out. I left as she asked. Getting on the phone, I called Mary Alice. She said that she would look out for the kids. It seemed like I was losing my meat quickly, and it was pissing me off. How the hell was I going to pull it off? I wanted to kill Jamie, but I didn't want to do that and not eat her. She looked infected, and I just could not bring myself to taste her flesh.

After leaving the shelter, I prepared a meal for Kale and Kyle then put them to sleep with a little Benadryl. Dressed in all black, I slipped out of the house around two-thirty in the morning, hoping Joyce wasn't out this time. I peeped out the window before I exited the apartment. As soon as my feet hit the cement, I began running like Forest Gump all the way to the shelter.

Arriving at the back door, it was propped open as always. Someone had placed a small rock in the doorway, so it wouldn't lock. I eased the door open and walked down the hallway to Mike and Michael's room. Before I opened the door, I took a deep breath. I didn't want to chance Jamie yelling and screaming at me, giving me away. As I opened the door, the two children were asleep, and Jamie was nowhere to be found. I opened the door wider and walked in. I looked up and down the hall, hoping I didn't get caught.

I woke up the kids. They were very sleepy. I carried Michael, as Mike walked slowly behind us. We eased out the back door, and I removed the rock, so the door would be locked. I took the kids down this woody path at the back of the facility. I couldn't chance being seen on the highway trying to get to the apartment. At the end of the path, I had to walk around to the front of the apartment with the kids. One car passed by, and I almost went into panic mode. I just prayed they didn't see me or the kids.

Opening the front door, I put both kids on the couch where they fell back to sleep immediately. I had Kool-Aid already made in the refrigerator, so I loaded it down with Benadryl. I woke each child up and told them to drink. I waited for about an hour and took Michael to the bathroom first. By this time, I had taken over my mother's room with the second bathroom. I pulled the garbage can in also. Walking into Kyle and Kale's room, I had to make sure they were still fast asleep.

I duct-taped Michael's mouth with Gorilla Tape, making sure he didn't scream and wake up the others. I began to slice Michael's body into pieces in the bathtub. I chose him first because he was fat, and it was going to take a while. I threw his feet and hands into the garbage. I decapitated the head from the body, and I threw it in the garbage too. After I had the parts separated, I cut the skin off the meat. Blood was coming out, so I had to stop the bleeding. After the bleeding stopped, I put them into individual grocery bags then placed them in one big, black garbage bag. Mary Alice had given me a small freezer for working so hard at the homeless shelter, so I put Michael in there. I locked the freezer door because I didn't want Mother to come back, stealing again. She would call the police on me for sure if she saw a dead child's body in here.

Now, it was time for Mike's turn. I did him the same way as Michael and placed him in the freezer too. After putting my favorite meat in the freezer, I had to bleach down the bathroom. Michael's feet had that immaculate smell as well. I sat right there on the bathroom floor and ate as much of his feet as I could. Smelling Mike's feet, they didn't have the smell I was searching for. After cleaning up myself, I took the garbage out to the dumpster, and placing bleach in the bags was perfect. The garbage truck was coming tomorrow, and that was a good thing. On my way back to the apartment, Joyce was sitting on the stairs, staring into space. I knew then that I was busted.

"What are you doing out? Are you sleeping with someone else?" she asked.

"No, I forgot to take the garbage out. I'm cleaning up."

"Don't lie to me, Reagus. I'm a big girl, so I can take it. If you don't want me, just let me know."

"Joyce, I'm not sleeping around on you. Don't you smell this bleach all over me? I told you that I'm cleaning up. I don't have enough time to clean because I go to school during the day and work in the evening. You know this," I explained, hoping she would shut up and leave me alone.

"I do smell the bleach all over you, and I'm so sorry for accusing you," she replied, as she tried to hug me, and I stepped backward.

"Are you excited?" I asked.

"Of course. I'm always excited when you're around. I want you so badly right now."

"Well, we can be together tomorrow night. I need to finish cleaning up and get some rest, so I can get up early for school. You need to be in the house too."

"Do you miss me?"

"Yes, I miss you, Joyce. So, get your butt up and go into the house. I'll please you tomorrow if you want," I replied, as I stood there and stared at her half-exposed body. I wanted to be with her at that moment, but I had more cleaning to do.

Joyce went inside the house and locked the door. I rushed into the house to finish cleaning up. I had to find a better way to do this. Sometimes, I felt like I was going to pass out from all the bleach. I was surprised that Mary Alice hadn't said anything about bottles of bleach missing from the facility. Hopefully, she didn't blame me.

After I wiped down the bathroom again, I proceeded to bed. I wasn't going to school the next day because my body was too tired. I hated missing school, but I had to. Plus, I couldn't wait to eat a piece of my favorite meat. Now, I had a month's supply of meat. We would eat it every day until it was all consumed.

The next morning came so fast. I got Kyle and Kale up, sending them off to school. As soon as they got on the bus, I began to prepare Michael's meat first. I also prepared potato salad with baked beans and sweet tea. After the food was prepared, I ate and ate until my stomach was about to burst.

After I let it all digest, I began cleaning the house again to make sure everything was in place. The twins were good about not being nosey, so that was a plus. They were the perfect siblings, but I had to make sure that Robin didn't come by. I asked the manager at the apartment complex to change the lock. They did so for a fee. Now, the only way Robin could get in was if she knocked or one of us let her in.

Arriving at the shelter that evening, Mary Alice was there, talking to Jamie. She demanded answers about her kids. I tried to avoid them, but it didn't work out that way. "Reagus, can you come in here please?" Mary Alice yelled through the doors.

"Yes, ma'am."

"Have you seen Mike and Michael? They seem to be missing."

"Yes, ma'am, I did. I was putting them to bed last night when Ms. Jamie came in and threw me out of the room. She slammed the door in my face, and that was the last I saw of them," I told

her, as Jamie looked at us, scratching at her arms and licking her lips.

"What was that all about, Jamie?" Mary Alice asked.

"I wanted to be alone with my kids," Jamie answered.

"I see. So, you are the last person to see the kids. Am I correct?"

"Yes, ma'am, but I left them in the room to sleep. I had to take care of some business," she struggled to say, as she continued scratching.

"I understand that, but you didn't wake someone up to watch them. You left your kids unattended and alone. I will have to call the police to help us find the children."

"Ms. Mary Alice, do you want me to go through the entire shelter and look for the children? There are so many places in here they could be," I insisted, knowing them two little boys were chilling at my house, one cooked and the other in the freezer, chilling, ready to be eaten.

"Call the police because I want some answers. Y'all need to give me my kids," Jamie yelled out.

Mary Alice called the police. Within five minutes, they came, rushing in. Mary Alice and I gave our statements. Other staff members came forward, saying Jamie was using drugs and leaving the kids anywhere she could. They took Jamie into

*custody. That was the last time I saw her. I do thank
her for giving me a month's supply of meals for my
family. I laughed deep down inside because her kid
tasted damn good.*

****

Dr. Amanda Smith asked, "Do you have any
abnormal fantasies that do not involve devouring
human flesh?"

"Abnormal fantasies are an understatement,"
I stated.

Occurred Incident: ABNORMAL CRACK POT

*Sitting at the Eddie M. Smith Student Union
eating my lunch, I overheard these two young boys
from Sardinian talking about this rotten cheese
from Sardinian sheep milk sheep that contained live
insect larvae called maggot cheese. The boys kept
going on and on about how much they loved the
cheese, so I decided to approach them.*

*"Excuse me, but I couldn't help but
overhear you two about this maggot cheese. It
seems like a delicacy. Where can I find it?" I
politely asked, hoping they didn't curse me out.*

*"Maggot cheese is so delicious," said the
taller, slim boy that looked like he tried to dye his
hair blonde.*

"Where can I find it?" I asked again.

93

"You cannot find maggot cheese in the United States. Because of the European food health regulation, cheese is forbidden, and many people have faced huge fines for violating the law," the much healthier boy stated, as he wiped his mouth.

"But you can get the Casu Marzu on the black market," the taller, slim boy said, as he shook his head.

"What is Casu Marzu?" I asked.

"That's the original name for the maggot cheese. But you do know that on the black market, they will probably charge you more because of the severity of it," the taller, slim boy said.

"I don't care about the money; I just want to taste the Casu Marzu. The way you two were talking about it, I thought you all had some I could taste," I stated, hoping they would share a piece of theirs with me.

"We didn't say we had any, or we would be eating it right now. Don't you think?" the heavier boy stated, as the two got up to walk off.

"My bad. I was just curious about the cheese."

"Check out Beecher's Handmade Cheese in New York City and ask for Adelasia, but don't tell him you got his name from us," the taller, slim boy said, as the two walked off.

Now, these two had me curious about this Casu Marzu. I went straight to the library and began researching maggot cheese. So many things came up, and I loved what I saw. There were YouTube videos about how to make it. The process began with a wheel of Pecorino Sardo Cheese. You placed the cheese out in the open, uncovered, and allowed these so-called cheese flies to lay eggs in the cheese. The eggs hatched into white maggots about eight millimeters long. My thoughts were, I have to have that cheese. It can't be that bad being that it is made from sheep's milk and infested with live maggots. What harm is that?

After that day of research, I became obsessed with the Casu Marzu. I could travel to New York to visit the restaurant that the two young Sardinian boys talked about. Mary Alice had left me enough money with the homeless shelter and my grandparents had left me all their money. The only thing that was stopping me from traveling there was me. I was a country boy that didn't know anything. Perhaps I should give the two Sardinian boys an offer they couldn't refuse.

A month had flown by, and I finally convinced the two Sardinian boys to help me retrieve the maggot cheese from the cheese factory in New York.

"Are you serious about helping me?" I asked the taller, slim boy.

"Yes, and my name is Bissente, but you can call me Vincent. That's my American name."

"And my name is Erricu, but my American name is Henrik," the heavier boy stated without even giving me eye contact.

"Okay, Vincent and Henrick, my name is Reagus. Now that we have learned each other's names, let's get down to business. When will we travel to New York to get my maggot cheese?" I demanded.

"Hold on, Reagus. It's not as easy as you think. As we stated before, the Casu Marzu is one of our Italian food customs that is illegal to produce and sell now," Vincent stated.

"You have told me that already, Vincent. I'm aware of it being illegal, but as you stated before, I could get it off the black market. Or you could get it from this Beecher's Handmade Cheese factory in New York. Either way, please help me. I have been craving it ever since I heard you two talking about it," I stated.

"Yes, young Reagus, we do understand. We have been drooling at the fact we might get another taste ourselves, but it's too expensive for us," Henrik replied, as he wiped his mouth.

"Well, Henrik, I am willing to buy myself a wheel of Casu Marzu and you two one each for yourselves. How do you like that deal? Plus, the $500 cash I am giving you two to help me."

"That's more than enough. We will make calls to Adelasia and go from there," Vincent advised.

We all departed from each other as if we had just made a big drug deal with the cartel. By this time, I'd purchased a small iPad and a cellphone from AT&T. The iPad kept me busy, looking at hundreds of videos on how to make maggot cheese and what it was supposed to look like. I had become so obsessed with getting this cheese that I began eating nothing but cheese. It took about two weeks for Henrik and Vincent to get back to me. I thought the two had taken my money and disappeared. They were sure to die if they had done me wrong, but one Friday evening, guess what? They brought me my maggot cheese.

Walking into my house in Sebastopol with this blue box in my hand, I was so excited and happy. I was finally getting a chance to taste this rare delicacy. Throwing my bookbag on the floor, I walked to the kitchen and gently placed the blue box down on the table. Carefully unwrapping my cheese, it looked hard. The smell was extremely sharp. I did as the videos showed me to carefully cut a hole at the top and lift it off like a lid. Lifting the lid, I could see the eight-millimeter-inch maggots traveling slowly throughout the cheese. Watching them moving about caused my penis to rise. I was just that excited.

Picking a piece of maggot cheese from its cradle, I put it in my mouth and chewed. The taste was like an extremely ripe gorgonzola but spicier. The spiciness was a bit overwhelming, but I continued to eat it. The texture of the cheese was very soft with some liquid seeping out. Also, being careful with the cheese, I placed the top of the maggot cheese back on because the YouTube videos stated when disturbed, the maggots could launch themselves fifteen centimeters. After consuming a few more bites, I decided to try another method that I saw in the videos. I placed the maggot cheese in a plastic bag and sealed it shut. My imagination got the best of me, and I wanted to experience it all at one time. After sealing the Ziploc bag shut, the maggots immediately began jumping from the cheese bread into the bag. The theory said that they starved from a lack of oxygen. After falling into the Ziploc bag, they died. It was incredible just to see how fast they died.

Removing the maggot-free cheese from the bag, I continued to eat some more of the cheese. It tasted better with the maggots. Luckily, I had a bottle of red wine that I mixed with human blood to chase it down. Consuming half of the maggot cheese, the smell became unbearable with such a strong odor that I didn't notice when I unwrapped the cheese. I guess I was so excited about tasting it that I didn't realize the smell. My mouth was left with a burning sensation, but nothing was too extreme.

After my experience with the Casu Marzu, I pulled off my clothes to take a cold shower. I felt very hot and annoyed for some reason. After undressing, I looked into the mirror at myself, and suddenly, I spotted a maggot hanging from my hair. Trying to grab it, it fell onto my nose and then leaped straight into my eye. I unfortunately didn't catch it. I tried washing out my eyes and putting Visine into them, but there were no results. The maggot had invaded my eye.

A week passed, and my eyes were swollen so hugely. I didn't know what to do but call Vincent and Henrik.

"What you mean one of the larvae invaded your eye?" Vincent stated over the phone as if he was in shock.

"That's exactly what I mean. I was eating Casu Marzu, and a maggot jumped on my face. I didn't feel it or see it until it went into my eye. And now, my eyes are very huge. I read articles about using goat meat to place on my eye to draw it out, but I don't have a clue where to get goat meat," I explained.

"Well, we can help you with that. There is a butcher up here by East Central that we go to for all our meats. We will go there, but you will have to come to the dorm," Vincent explained.

*"I don't want to come out in public with my
eye this huge. There is no way. I need you guys to
come here to my house. Do you know where
Sebastopol is?" I asked.*

*"Yes, we do. We have conducted a few
speeches at Sebastopol Attendance Center. Are you
near there?" Vincent asked me.*

*"Yes, I am right behind it. My house looks
like it is haunted." I laughed.*

*"And you find that funny?" Vincent
remarked.*

*"Yes, I do find it funny. Everyone that
passes by here thinks so. But anyway, can you
please hurry up and come help me?" I pleaded.*

*"Okay, Reagus, but you owe me. We
explained to you that you would have to wear some
type of eye equipment to protect your eyes. We all
watched the videos repeatedly on how they can
launch up to fifteen centimeters," Vincent
explained.*

*"I know all that, Vincent. Just come over
and I have money to pay you," I harshly stated, as I
hung the phone up in his face. I texted my address
to his phone, hoping that he had a GPS.*

*My thoughts were to kill his ass as soon as
he helped me get this maggot out of my eye.
Reading the leading articles, there could be more
than one now since I had waited an entire week.*

After pacing for about two hours, Vincent finally showed up. He was dressed strangely. He had on all black. I guess he hadn't realized that it was hot outside.

"It's about time you showed up," I remarked with my hand over my eye.

"Well, I got here as fast as I could. You do realize that school is about to end. And I had to wait until the butcher opened. Everything doesn't just happen on your time," Vincent smarted off and walked up to the door.

"Welcome to my rental."

"This is a scary-looking house you have here. I would have never thought twice to stop by here," he joked.

"I don't ever have company. Everyone is so afraid of this house. This is just an old house that needs a little TLC."

"Well, you aren't doing a good job," he joked again with a smirk on his face.

"Anyway, Vincent, what can you do about this?" I spoke, as I took my hand down from my eye, and he stepped back with a blank expression on his face.

"What have you done to yourself?"

"I haven't done anything. It's been about a week since the maggot got into my eye. I tried to use a regular piece of meat to draw it out but nothing,"

*I explained, as I walked to the kitchen, and Vincent
followed.*

*"You do realize that there could be so many
in there that I can't help you. From the looks of
your eye, it's more than one," Vincent whispered,
as he continued to stare at my eye in disbelief.*

*"Just please do the best that you can. I
would appreciate it."*

*"Sit down and let me see how bad it is. I
don't understand why you didn't tell me the same
day it happened. I don't think you would have been
this miserable."*

*"I wanted to do it myself, and yes, I am very
miserable," I explained, as I held my head back,
and Vincent lifted my eyelid, looking around. He
was looking all around and at the top with his
mouth open. His breath smelled like ass, causing me
to want to vomit.*

*"Wow, Reagus, there is more than one
maggot in there. It's unbelievable. I've never seen it
that severe," Vincent stated, as he continued to look
into my eye.*

*Quickly pushing him away, I began to vomit.
I put my hands over my mouth and rushed to the
garbage can that was nearby. It seemed like I was
throwing up my brain. My eye began to pound very
badly. Wiping my mouth, I sat down, as Vincent
took the goat meat from its package. It wasn't a
clean piece of meat but bloody.*

"Why is that meat bloody like that?" I
asked, putting my hand over my eye.

"Because it's goat meat. Just move your
hand," he ordered.

"Well, doesn't look normal to me."

"Maggots in your eye aren't normal either,
but you have them." He smarted off again.

Tilting my head backward, Vincent placed
the bloody goat meat over my eye. I held onto the
goat meat and began to feel my eye tingling. As we
sat there, waiting, one by one, the maggots were
exiting my eye. Ten maggots were laying on the
goat meat. Vincent immediately placed the goat
meat with live maggots into a Ziploc bag. He sealed
the bag, and a few minutes later, all ten of them lay
dead.

"How do you know they are all gone from
my eye?" I asked Vincent, as he stared at the
maggots in the Ziploc bag.

"I don't know, but we will see. If your eye
goes down, then you are safe, but if your eye
continues to be swollen, then you need to try this
method again or go to a professional," he stated.

"I don't feel anything moving around
anymore, and my eye feels a lot better," I explained.

"I am glad to hear I helped you," he spoke,
as he held out his hand. I knew that he wanted
money.

"How much?"

"Two hundred dollars is good."

"Two hundred dollars? All you did was put a piece of goat meat on my eye, and that's it."

"Well, I did take the time out of my busy day to come and help you. I didn't have to do that," he spoke, as he picked up the Ziploc bag.

"You're right," I replied, as I walked into the living room and took the money off the table. Instead of giving him two hundred, I gave him three hundred. I continued, "Here is three hundred. That's more than two."

"Yes, it is, and I thank you. Now, take care of your eye," Vincent ordered before he walked out my front door.

"Thank you," I stated to myself.

After that day, my eye went down and was back to normal. Once a month when I ordered maggot cheese from Adalesia, who worked at Beecher's in New York City, I wore goggles. That experience with maggots in my eye was horrible. That was a learning experience I would never forget.

CHAPTER 5

(Older & Hungrier)

Dr. Amanda Smith asked, "When did you decide to start killing victims from the college? These kids had families; you weren't afraid of getting caught?"

"After the killing of my first couple of victims, I did fear getting caught, but that didn't stop me. My cravings for human flesh grew greater than I imagined. I had developed a taste for the kills. Cravings to hurt people violently," I answered.

Occurred Incident: HUNGRY FOR MORE

After I got out of the mental institution, Robin signed me up for GED classes. She didn't know if I could read or write. She didn't know if I had the education to test out. I thank God for the lady in the mental institution for teaching me. She knew I wasn't crazy. She knew I wasn't supposed to be there. Just a young child with no guidance. I spent a couple of months in the GED program when I got home. That spring, I got my GED, then I spent two more years in college.

After I graduated from East Central Community College with an associate degree in nursing, things were beginning to look up for me. In my second year at EC, I began to work part-time at this doctor's office in Decatur but still worked at the homeless shelter on the weekends. Mary Alice showed me how to drive because I bought myself a new 2000, red Chevy Tahoe.

I had put up a tin wall all around the two-acre property my grandparents left me. It cost me almost ten grand, but I wanted to keep my family and other unwanted guests out. I didn't talk to my family because they all thought I was weird and nuts. So many people tried to bring me down, and it didn't happen. I was determined to make something of my life, even though I couldn't hide the truth of who I was and what I wanted to do.

Over the years, I was still messing off with Joyce. She got pregnant during my second semester at East Central. She ended up having a baby boy named Brady. She wanted me to use my last name, but I didn't want him to have Raymond Dune's last name, so she ended up giving Brady her last name. She hated me for that and wouldn't let me see him half the time. It didn't matter because I didn't care. He would just get in the way of my plans to have freezers and freezers of my favorite meat.

For the first time in years, I finally got a chance to eat my favorite meat again. I was chilling at a college football game, and two white girls I knew from East Central approached me, wanting to get high. I had a few bags of weed on me. They looked good, so I invited them back to my house. I advised them to leave their car on the East Central campus; I would bring them back because I had to attend class early that morning.

We got high on the way back to my house through Lake, Mississippi. I had learned my way around since I got my new car. Pulling up at my gate; I got out and unlocked it. One of the girls pulled my car in. I locked us in, and we continued up.

All three of us sat around, smoking weed. The girls got hungry, so I cooked. I whipped up some buttered mashed potatoes with chicken wings. I put opioids in the mashed potatoes, so they wouldn't be detected by them. I knew that opioids would numb them, and then respiratory failure would seal the deal. The pills were crushed earlier that day after I left the doctor's office. I had stolen so many drugs that it looked like I had a pharmacy in my closet. I had stolen opioids, tricyclics, chloroform, benzene, and much, much more. It was so easy, like stealing candy from a baby. The doctor was a country bumpkin and believed everyone was innocent.

Anyway, we all sat down to eat. I just ate chicken. Those two females ate up all the mashed potatoes. My face lit up because I was waiting on the drug to put their asses to sleep, but instead, it took a turn. The blonde head girl started complaining of chest pains. She began to breathe

*hard and tried to cry out. As her body fell to the
floor, the brunette did the same thing. Both of their
bodies lay on my floor.*

*Immediately, I jumped up and checked for a
pulse under the neck of both girls. I let out laughter
that got my cock hard. Dragging both bodies into
the living room, I put on some porn. I undressed
and then cut off their clothes. As I sat back down,
my cock grew harder. I began to stroke myself, as
they lay there. Jumping down on the floor, I began
to suck the breast of the blonde girl. Damn, she
tasted so good. Looking up at the porn, I just jacked
off right there on her face. Her eyes were wide open
and pierced me with an evil look.*

*After ejaculating, I got a wagon and rolled
both females into the slaughterhouse. Carefully
hanging the first body, suddenly, one of the girls
jumped up, screaming. She was looking wild. Her
eyes looked so big, and her skin was glossy. She
jumped up, running to the door, exiting. I
immediately grabbed the axe and ran after her. She
was at my gate, trying to take the lock off with her
hands. No words escaped her lips until she saw me
running up to her with the axe. She then began
climbing my black gate, trying to escape. I hit her in
the back with the axe. She fell to the ground like a
brick. Pulling the axe from her back, I hit her dead
in the head. Cutting her body up to pieces right
there on sight, I broke out in a sweat. Every crack*

of her bone was a sweet sound to me. After slicing her to pieces, I almost cried because I messed up my favorite meat. I went to the house and retrieved a red rock crape tree and planted it with her body parts underneath.

Afterwards, I went to the barn and finished with the other girl. I sliced and sliced her into pieces. Nobody would know because my folks slaughtered hogs. Tomorrow was going to be perfect to cover up because they had talked to me about slaughtering a hog for meat. Washing each piece of meat, I bagged it. I sliced off the ass cheeks of the brunette female and began eating right there. I scooped it out and chewed. It had no smell and no taste. Her ass cheeks melted like a piece of sweet tuna. Running into the house, I gathered some Saltine crackers and ran back to finish my feast. I felt like I was in Heaven.

After bagging and tagging every bag of meat, I washed down the machine with the water hose. I started a big barn fire in the backyard. There was a brown rusty barrel in the back, so I took the bloody clothes, cell phones, and any other evidence out back, burning it. Pouring gas on it, the fire jumped higher. I had to make sure that everything burned to a crisp.

About an hour later, the fire burned down. I stood out, naked, for a few minutes because I had to toss my clothes in the fire as well. It was cold outside, but my adrenaline was high. It felt like I had no feelings at all. My mind went back to my meat; I had to hurry back and finish those ass cheeks. I finished up my meal then put the bags of my favorite meat into the big freezers my grandparents had in the garage. They had about four big freezers out there. When I first moved in, I had to get rid of that old meat. I issued out plenty to my family and even dropped bags off to Kyle and Kale. Robin begged for money, but I wasn't letting her have anything. She turned her back on me, and now I shall turn my back on her.

Cleaning up the living room, I began to watch more porn. I wanted to jack off again, but I didn't have the urge. Walking into the kitchen and opening the refrigerator, I took out the girl's brain. Instantly, my cock jumped hard. I sat her brain on the table and beat off to the porn. The porn sounded loud from the television, but I stared at the brain on the table facing me. Closing my eyes, I thought about how I chopped them down and bagged them. My cock shot off into the air so hard. It took a few seconds before all the juices had disappeared.

I cleaned up with Comet and went to bed. All I could think about was eating the flesh of that meat. I couldn't risk getting more students from the school because too many eyes were lurking. There were too many people and too many cameras.

Mary Alice had died. I knew that my time had run out at the homeless shelter. Mary Alice let me run in and out as I pleased, but the new person was probably going to be very strict.

After Mary Alice was buried, her will was read. She had given me the "Forest Stewpot" homeless shelter. I just smiled, but deep down inside, I was jumping for joy. My mind wondered repeatedly how to get more meat. Then, it hit me; nobody would notice if the homeless were missing. I had found a way to eat my favorite meat every single day – the homeless shelter.

I made it home and poured myself a glass of Moët wine while eating a piece of brain I had stored in the refrigerator. My Uncle Earl had come up to check on me. I had given him some of the chicken I had left over from the other night. He was drinking straight vodka like it was water. We talked and talked shit to each other, then he discovered my food. He wanted to taste what I was eating. I had fried a section that morning before Mary Alice's funeral.

"What are you eating on, boy?" Uncle Earl asked.

"Why? You want a piece?"

"Shit, it looks good. I would like to try it."

"Here, eat a piece," I replied, as I put a piece of the brain on his plate. He didn't even

examine the meat; Uncle Earl just swallowed it whole.

"Damn, boy, that shit tastes good. Give me another piece."

"You're going to get addicted," I joked.

"I don't give a damn."

"Okay," I replied, as I let him finish up the brain. I continued, "You know Mary Alice gave me the homeless shelter downtown. I'm the sole owner of it."

"Damn, boy, you got it going on. You going to give me a job?" he asked.

"Yes, I am. Your job is to make sure that the slaughterhouse is cleaned weekly. I mean, keep it clean. Bleach, Purex, or whatever it takes."

"That's it? I can do that."

"Good. I will feed you every day, and whatever you see here on Jersey Joe Patrick Estates, stays here on Jersey Joe Patrick Estates. I don't need you running around here bragging about what I do for my property. I will have you set up for life without having to work at all."

"Damn, boy, you got it like that?"

"Yes, I do. Just stick with me and you will never go hungry or broke again," I said.

We lifted our bottles in the air, and I spoke, "I get to eat my favorite meat every single day, and nobody can stop me now. That homeless shelter is all mine."

After that day, no homeless person was safe. I didn't discriminate; I was going to eat them all one by one.

****

Dr. Amanda Smith asked, "Did killing your victims become a sport, or was it solely for eating the human flesh?"

"But killing my prey had become a sport when I found out that their skin was damaged. Who wants to eat damaged meat? There were three that I can mention off the top of my head that I killed for the sport after discovering scars and burns. I became so angry with these people after discovering their damage. So angry and violent, I wanted them to feel my pain. The thrill of mutilating a person gave me a massive hard-on," I answered.

Occurred Incident: *BRAZEN GRILL*

"Why are you doing this to me, you fucking asshole?" the short-haired, brunette male student I had kidnapped from school yelled, as he was trying to struggle to get out of the rope I had tied him up in.

"You have such harsh words for me, young man. I would advise you not to call me names. And, for the record, I am not gay. Did you think I wanted you sexually?" I laughed, as I walked over to him, as he lay stretched out on my kitchen floor. I had

drugged him, stripped him naked, and tied him up to an iron pole. He was stretched out like a dead deer that was about to be cleaned and eaten.

"Why else would you have me tied up, naked? You need to get me out of this. Once I get free, I am going to kill you with my bare hands," the boy threatened.

"You can't be serious. You're not going to get free, and you're not going to kill me." I laughed in his face. I continued, "What is your name?"

"I'm not telling you shit. Untie me right now or else," he threatened again.

"Or else what? I'm trying to make conversation with you, but you're starting to piss me off. Again, what's your name?"

"My name is Go Fuck Yourself," he yelled, as he tried to spit at me but didn't make it far.

"Well, Mr. Go Fuck Yourself, I see you will die tonight. I was going to let you live for a few days and make you suffer, but you deserve the death penalty," I stated, as I grabbed the iron pole he was tied to and began dragging him out my back door.

"I don't want to die. Please don't kill me. My name is Billy. Just please don't kill me," he screamed, as I continued to drag him to this huge-looking barbecue grill I had my Uncle Earl build especially for this occasion. This specially made grill was built from three iron barrels. All three were welded together.

"Well, Billy, it's surely a fine time to want to have a conversation with me. I tried to be nice to you, but you didn't want to be nice. Now, you're about to die, and you want to talk. I don't have any conversation for you right now. I'm all out of words," I replied, as I dropped his body to the ground and began preparing my fire with my huge barbecue grill.

"I apologize. Please just don't kill me. What do you want from me? My family has money if that's what you want. Just please don't kill me," Billy begged.

"I don't care about money. When I saw your face, I fell in love with your skin. It was so tight and well taken care of. But when you pulled off your shirt walking through the campus, I almost vomited on myself seeing those nasty scars all over your body like that. What happened to it?"

"Just untie me and I will tell you any and everything you want to know."

"You will tell me anyway. You can keep wishing because I'm not going to untie you. So, again, what happened to your skin?"

"Just please untie me. I promise I won't try anything," he begged.

"Well, that's it for the small talk, Billy," I replied, as I poured a little gas on the wood logs that were under the old-fashioned barbecue grill.

"What are you going to do with that? I know you don't expect me to get in there. Oh, my God, you're going to burn me alive." Billy began yelling and screaming. Tears rolled down his face, as he begged me not to do it.

"I tried to talk to you, but you didn't care about my conversation."

"Don't you dare put me in there, you fucking asshole." He screamed between his cries.

"You sure have a thing for name-calling," I stated, just as I began to kick him over and over with so much rage. After a few minutes of me kicking him, he passed out. I continued talking to his unconscious body. "I can't believe you let this happen to your body like this."

As Billy lay there on the ground, I adjusted the big field light I had shining on the big old-fashioned barrels. Now, trying to lift Billy's body into it was harder than I imagined. He weighed at least one hundred sixty-five pounds. I struggled for about fifteen minutes, trying to get his body to fall in. As soon as his body hit the bottom of the barrel, he began to wake up. His torso was facing downward.

"Hey, man, don't do this to me. I have a family that loves me. You can't possibly want to do this to me," he spoke, as he tried to struggle against the rope that had him bound.

"I don't care about you or your family. Your skin is damaged, and there is nothing I can do with you," I stated, as I closed the lid down and secured it with a master key lock. I went down to his feet and secured that end as well. The barrel was so huge that I had to have two doors.

Billy was screaming like a little girl but was muffled by the iron barrel. I pulled a small box of matches from my pocket. Striking it, I threw it on the gas logs.

"No, please, help me," Billy screamed and screamed. I could hear his body bouncing around in the barrel. After a few minutes of suffering, he was dead. No more screams were escaping from his mouth. Billy was dead.

Standing there, staring at the barrel for about an hour, I decided to go inside the house. I laughed my ass off at the screams I'd heard from Billy. He was a big badass at first then turned into a little girl begging. Closing my back door, I walked over to the small kitchen window above the sink and looked out one last time. The fire was still burning the body. It was probably ashes now. I felt tired, so I took a shower then retired to bed, not caring about Billy's burned body. I hoped he rotted in hell.

Laying in bed, staring at the ceiling, I thought about how easy it was to kidnap Billy. These college kids were making it so easy for me. My memory faded back to me being at the Chevron, drinking a Bud Light beer. This funny-looking kid from my class walked into the store. I immediately recognized him as the boy with scars all over his body. He was the boy I wanted to punish. He shouldn't treat his skin like that.

After a few minutes, the boy came out of the store. I had my window down and spoke, "Hey, I remember you from one of my classes. You walked over here?" I asked, knowing damn well I saw him walk from across the street.

"Yep, I remember you from class. And yep, I walked."

"I can give you a ride back to the campus since it's right there." I invited.

"No thanks. The dorm is just right there," he stated.

"Okay, I got Bud Light beer," I stated, as I held up my beer to show him.

"Oh, hell yeah." He grinned, as he made his way to my passenger seat.

"Drink up," I offered, as I handed him a cold bottle of Bud Light. He immediately drank it down like a fish. From the look of it, he was thirsty.

"You must have needed that beer." I laughed.

"Hell yeah. I have been studying so hard all week for these classes. Man, if you only knew," he stated, as he finished up the beer.

"I know exactly what you're talking about. You want another one?" I offered, as I took the bottle from him and gave him another one. I continued, "Which dorm do you live in?"

"I live in Newsome Hall."

"Okay, I live in Neshoba Hall, but my mom will tell you differently. Since I stay at home all the time, she doesn't think I live on campus." I laughed, chugging my beer.

"I probably would live at home if I was in the area. I'm from Gulfport."

"That's on the Mississippi Coast, right?"

"Yep."

"That's a long way from home," I stated, as I cranked up the car to drive over to Newsome Hall, hoping that campus police didn't spot us. This was not the time to go to jail.

"How far do you live from here?" he asked.

"Maybe about twenty minutes from here. It's not that long of a drive," I answered.

"Okay, that's not too bad of a drive."

"No, it's not. My mom probably wished it was farther away."

We both laughed and continued drinking our beers, as we made it to Newsome Hall. I found a parking spot in the back. We sat there, talked, and drank beer. I bought two twelve-pack bottles, and we had already finished one box. We had started working on the second box when Billy passed out in my car. He was drinking like he had never tasted beer before, and I let him drink. I needed him to be easy, and he was. After getting him back to my house, it was smooth sailing after that. And now, he suffered a violent death.

I laughed and laughed at Billy's cries until I fell asleep. The next day, I went out and gathered his ashes from the barrel and planted a red rock crape tree in his memory.

Occurred Incident: BURIED EXECUTION

"Hello, Mother, didn't think I would ever see you again," I stated to Robin, as I opened the black gate to let her and her boyfriend enter my property.

"There is no such thing. I am your mother. Of course you would see me again," she lied, as John drove on up to the house, as I locked the gate back.

I walked up to the house after the two didn't give me a ride, and they stood out, admiring my grandparents' old house. It was a nice brick house they left me. I didn't bother changing anything because I loved the memories, especially my killings.

"So, where is this money you promised to give me?" Robin stated right off the back with a mean look on her face. She looked so torn down. Her blonde hair was now brunette after dying it.

She had sores all over her arms and face. Robin was looking like a full-blown crackhead now.

"Robin, be patient. I have the money. I didn't know that you were just going to take the money and disappear from me. Can you at least have a little dinner with me?" I asked nicely. She looked over at John, who was staring at me. I continued, "John, you two please have dinner with me. I still have the 2,000 dollars I am going to give you."

"Robin, I thought you said it was 1,500 dollars Reagus was giving us." He directed it to her.

"Reagus did say $1,500."

"I did say $1,500.00, but I was giving Robin the extra $500 to buy Kyle and Kale food and clothes," I lied, as I took the money out of my front right pocket. Just as I thought, both of their eyes got very big. I could see the greed in their hearts.

"Hell yeah, we can have dinner," John stated, as he ran around the truck and grabbed Robin's hand, guiding her up to the front door. I followed behind them.

"Great. So happy you could convince her to stay for a little. I miss her," I lied again, hoping they would eat up my lies just as quickly as I threw them out.

"Well, I don't have all day to be here, Reagus," Robin shot back, as she opened the door and entered the house first.

"We have all the time in the world. You just go ahead and shut your mouth," John threatened her, as we all walked into the kitchen. "Something smells good," he stated.

"I cooked you two a huge T-Bone steak with mashed potatoes, seared shrimp with cheese sauce, and broccoli. Hope you two enjoy it," I replied with a smirk on my face.

"You did miss your mama. Shit, did you miss me too?" John laughed, as the two sat down at the table.

"I missed you both, how about that? Everything is done. I can fix your plates," I offered, as I gathered the plates and began preparing them. They both watched me like a hawk.

"What made you prepare us a meal and offer to give us money after we begged you when you first got it?" Robin shot at me.

"Because it was looking like I was greedy, and honestly, I was hoping that you let me visit Kyle and Kale. I miss them so much and want to spend time with them. Where are they at anyway?" I asked.

"They are somewhere around here making trouble for themselves," she remarked, and John pushed her.

"Don't talk about my babies like that. They are good kids." He probably lied. I had heard that the two were going around stealing and robbing people blind.

"Can I please see them?" I asked again, as I placed the plates down in front of them with A-1 Sauce.

"Yes, you can see them," John answered, and Mother just shrugged her shoulders, as she dug into the steak.

They both began eating without anything else to say. I took out the money and placed it on the counter in front of them. If they saw the money, they wouldn't be so anxious to leave. Getting out two glasses, I opened a bottle of my special wine mixed with blood and served them a glass. Sitting the bottle in front of them, they drank it very fast. I sat down with them and began eating my steak but no potatoes. Their potatoes and wine were laced with hydrocodone and lunexor pills. I crushed them very fine before Robin and John came over. Hopefully, they would go down soon.

"Hope you two are enjoying dinner?" I asked them both, hoping one of them showed a sign of the pills kicking in.

"Boy, you know how to cook a good steak, and these potatoes are excellent," John remarked, as he finished up his meal and drank down the last bit of wine.

"Why you drank all the damn wine?" Robin snapped at John.

"It tasted so good. Never had that kind of wine before."

"Hold on, Robin. I have another bottle," I interrupted, as I took out the second bottle of wine. Something told me that it was going to take a minute to down these two on their asses. Pouring her another glass of wine, John got up from the table and stretched.

"I haven't had a good meal like that in such a long time. Shit, I think I might need a nap before we leave out." He yawned, looking over at the money.

"You need a nap. For what?" Robin snapped.

"That was a good meal, and you know it."

I interrupted. "I learned to cook over the years."

"I just bet you did," Robin remarked, as she reached over and grabbed the money.

"You need to count it to see if I shortchanged you?" I laughed.

"You're right. I don't know about you," she snapped back.

"Robin, why would I have cooked you a good meal and not given you the money I said I was going to give you? I'm not like that anymore," I

lied, wondering why she hadn't gotten sleepy. I wondered why the drugs weren't affecting her.

"I don't know what you are capable of doing," she replied to me.

"Whatever. Anyway, John, you can take a nap on the couch if you want to, or you two can go. Seems like Mother doesn't want to stay here any longer with me," I spoke.

"Sit your ass down, Robin. The boy gave you the money and cooked you a good meal," John stated, as he worked his way over to the couch in the living room. He stuck his hands down his pants, grabbed his crotch, and fell asleep quickly.

"You two must have been up for a long time. John is out sleep already," I spoke.

"John, get your ass up. We must go," Robin yelled, as she walked over to him and began shaking him violently.

"Just leave him alone and let him sleep. You can't possibly be in such a big hurry," I yelled at her and then began cleaning up the kitchen.

"Shut the hell up, Reagus," she grunted, as she flopped down next to him.

I didn't say another word to her but continued cleaning the kitchen. After a few minutes, I saw they both were asleep, just like I planned. I poured out the rest of the pill-infested mashed potatoes and wine. After cleaning the kitchen with bleach, I went into John's pocket and got out the *keys to their car. Driving the car to the back of the property through the woods, I covered it with the top of pine trees I had cut down back there.*

Making it back to the house, I noticed that John wasn't on the couch where I left him. Robin had stretched out on the couch. Walking through the house slowly, I checked every room. Where in the hell could John be? As I passed the bathroom door, it flew open, and John, barely moving, made his way back to the couch. I walked slowly behind him, not saying a word.

He lay down on the couch next to Robin. I had to act fast. I didn't realize the two would be able to move at all. Perhaps, their bodies were used to more intense drugs that only had a little effect on them. Running to the back room, I gathered rope, pruners, and an eight-inch chef knife and prepared for their death.

As John and Robin sat on the back porch, tied up in chairs, I gathered my water hose with my new XL-stream firehouse nozzle attached. Stripping them of their clothes, John had Gorilla Tape across his mouth, and Robin was free to scream whenever I began to torture her. Turning the nozzle toward Mother and spraying the jet stream, her head bounced up, as she screamed for me to set her free.

"Reagus, what the hell are you doing?" she screamed, as she tried to shake the water from her face.

"Well, you were sleeping, and I was helping you wake the hell up." I slowly spoke with a nasty grin on my face.

"Untie me right now. And where are my clothes? Why are you doing this to us?" She asked questions back-to-back.

"So many questions, Mother. I can answer them one by one if you like. Your clothes are over there until my barbecue grill is ready for me to burn. That's one question. Untying you isn't an option, and the third question, I am doing this because I have prepared to kill you and John. You two have been my worst enemies."

"Reagus, please don't do this," she begged.

"Don't beg me, Robin, because it will make me kill you faster." I smiled.

"How can you kill your mother? You are sicker than I thought," she harshly stated.

"You should know why. You were never a good mother to me, Robin. And you let those people take me away. I was only a child, and you didn't care. They tortured me in that horrible place, and you did nothing. You visited me a few times, and that's it. You didn't bother to check on me. You didn't want me anymore is what the people used to tell me. How could a mother leave her child in an awful place like that? How, Robin?" I yelled at her and threw the water hose onto the ground. I had

reached the point of anger just thinking about the incidents that happened to me.

"I didn't have no ride to come see you, and you knew that. I wanted to come, but nobody would take me. You know that I love you and wanted to see you," she lied. The expression on her face told me she was lying.

"Robin, you don't love anyone but yourself and John. Your children suffered because you were a whore chasing down the crack and that no-good John. If you had been a good mother, Amber Rose would still be alive. I had to kill her and eat her because she would have suffered in this world as I did. Well, of course, I was hungry. Kale and Kyle were starving to death, so I killed Amber Rose and cooked her. She tasted very delicious," I stated, as I walked over to Robin and stared her directly in the face.

"You're a sick bastard. I knew you killed Amber Rose. John, wake up. Reagus killed her; he killed Amber Rose," Robin yelled out to John, who was still unconscious

"He's not waking up anytime soon, so you can stop talking to him. This is a conversation between a mother and son. See, we can't have a conversation amongst each other without you wanting to put John in our business. John is irrelevant to me. He will die fast, unlike you." I *stated, as I picked up the pruner and sat down on the porch next to Robin.*

"What are you going to do with that? Don't you dare touch me with those things!" she screamed at me.

"These here, Robin, are pruners. I have prepared to help you remove your awful-smelling toes." I grabbed at her feet, and she tried to grip them tightly.

"Please don't do this. I'm your mother," she hollered out.

"You being my mother is a very bad thing," I spoke, as I placed the pruner to her toes and began cutting them off one by one. Listening to her scream and beg was music to my ears. I took my time and pruned them. After decapitating her toes, I noticed John was awake and trying to break free from his chair. I said, "Well, looks like John is awake. Maybe he wants to join in on the fun."

"Reagus," Robin softly spoke between sobs.

"Shut up. I've decided that we are going to play a game. I ask questions, and you answer. If I feel like you are lying, I will stab John. If I feel you are telling the truth, I won't stab you.. Now, let's play," I spoke, as I stood up with the bloody pruners in my hand. Dropping them on the porch, I picked up the eight-inch chef knife.

"I'm not answering no questions," Robin stated.

"Yes, you will answer every single question because if you don't, I will bury you alive in that coffin. I will leave you there for the ants to eat at you slowly." I pointed to this shallow grave with this wooden box sitting next to it. Uncle Earl made it just for this occasion.

"You can't possibly be this sick to torture your mother. I am your mother. You will untie me right now," she ordered, as tears escaped her face.

"Question number one: did you ever love me?"

"Reagus, don't do this."

"Question number one, Robin: did you ever love me?" I asked again with a little bass in my voice. My heart was pounding fast because I knew deep down, she didn't love me, but I wanted her to.

"Yeah, I loved you." She spoke and turned her head, not looking at me.

"Liar," I screamed, as I pulled back the knife and stabbed John straight in the foot. Mother jumped, as John tried to scream through his taped mouth. Stabbing him and pulling the knife out quickly, I said, "You are a liar, Robin. Now, let's try this again."

"I'm your mother. Why do you think I don't love you?" She spoke this time, staring into my face.

"Because, Robin, you let those people hurt me. You didn't fucking care about me," I yelled, as

I jumped up on the porch, looking down into her sad face.

"I do love you," Robin softly spoke.

"Liar," I screamed again, as I stabbed her in the thigh. The knife went into her leg with so much force that her entire body shook so hard. She screamed so loudly that it almost burst my eardrum. Pulling the knife from her leg, I asked another question. "Why did you take my father away from me? You knew I loved him more than you, and you took him away. Why?"

Robin sat in the chair for a few minutes in agony. She stared down at her toes and then back at me. I knew she was trying to cook up a good lie to tell me.

"Raymond was my pimp. He was selling drugs, and I needed what he had, so I had sex for drugs. In the process, you came along," Robin whispered, as she held up her right leg, staring at the blood and her missing toes.

"Well, damn, you finally told the truth for once. I'm impressed."

"Reagus, please stop this. I am going to bleed to death if I don't get help. Please," Robin begged, as she looked over at John. His eyes were big and yellow. It looked like he had jaundice.

"Next question: why didn't you visit me in that hell hole like any other parent is supposed to do for their child? I was alone and afraid to go to

sleep at night. Do you have any idea what those monsters did to me in there?" I remarked, hoping she would say something.

Robin shook her head in the no position and held her head back. I started to just go ahead and cut her throat, but I needed answers.

"Answer the question," I demanded, as I took the prunes and moved closer to John's toes. I was going to prune them just like I did hers.

"Please don't, Reagus. I don't know why I didn't come. I guess drugs," Robin honestly stated.

"Drugs."

"Yes, drugs."

"And there is more. Drugs couldn't have possibly kept you away from your child, Robin."

"And John told me to just leave you there and hopefully you would die. He said we didn't want you anyway, so I didn't come to see you. If I had, he would have beat my ass," Robin honestly stated again.

Looking at John, I spoke. "So, you told Robin that I would eventually die in there, huh?"

John began shaking his head and staring at me. I placed the prunes down on the porch, and grabbing the knife, I began sawing his toes apart from his body. The screams soared through the clear Gorilla Tape I placed on his mouth. After decapitating the first foot, I decided to remove the

*tape from his mouth. I needed to hear the screams
escaping from his filthy, drug mouth.*

*"Leave him alone, Reagus," Robin
screamed, as I grabbed his other foot and began
sawing away with my knife. Taking my time slowly,
I sawed one toe at a time, and John fainted. His
head fell backward as if he was dead.*

*"John! John! John!" Robin shouted out, but
there was no movement.*

"I'll wake him up." I laughed.

*"Stop this madness, Reagus. I didn't raise
you to become a monster."*

*"Robin, you didn't raise me at all. The
people at East Mississippi Mental Institution raised
me. How dare you take the credit?" I scorned.*

*"I did raise you until your tenth birthday.
Don't say I never had any part in your upbringing,"
she remarked.*

*"Seems like you didn't do a good job. Look
at me now." I laughed again.*

"You're sick."

*"Not as sick as Raymond Dune. Did you
know he liked having sex with children?" I shocked
her.*

*"Raymond isn't like that. Stop lying like
that," Robin shouted at me.*

*"He confessed just before I killed him. He
said that he would have done me too."*

"You killed Raymond?" she asked, as the color from her face disappeared. She looked like she had seen a ghost.

"Well, technically, I didn't kill him. Some animals in the woods killed him. The only thing I did was chop his legs off, so he wouldn't be able to walk out of anybody else's life. But I bet his other children are glad I killed him. He was probably doing them all. To think about it, did you ever let him touch Kale or Kyle?"

"Don't ask me that," Robin spoke, as she looked away with a guilty look on her face.

"So, you did let Raymond Dune have sex with them? Tell me," I shouted so loud that she jumped. The anger had gone from zero to one hundred now. How could a mother offer her child to a man for drugs?

"Just Kale. She didn't care. She knew I needed help," Robin whispered.

"You let Raymond Dune have sex with Kale. She is only a child. What do you mean she didn't care? You can't possibly be serious," I screamed at her, as John began to wake up.

"Reagus, I need help. I know I'm a sick mother, but I needed those drugs," she explained.

"You're telling me that you sold your child to a man for drugs and her..." I trailed off.

Throwing the knife on the ground, I grabbed John's chair and flipped him backward. His body crashed into the porch, as he screamed out. Dragging him off the porch onto the ground, his body gave out a loud thump. I dragged him over by this coffin I had just for Robin.

"Please, Reagus, don't kill me. Please don't kill me. You can go ahead and kill Robin. I promise I won't say a word to the police," John begged, as I grabbed the axe handle.

"This is all your fault," I shouted, as I lifted the axe and began whaling on John. Chop after chop, I severed his body into pieces. The chair had broken from so much force. Human meat was flying all over the place. I was angry. No, I was pissed.

"Reagus, stop it. You're killing him," Robin screamed with fear.

"That's my point – to kill him," I calmly replied, as I continued to sever his head from his body. Kicking his head to the side, I took all my anger out on John's mutilated body. I chopped until I was damn near tired. Blood and guts were all over my green grass. Silence filled my ears, as I severed his body into a thousand pieces. Suddenly, I heard Robin screaming.

"Shut up. Just shut the hell up, you freaking whore," I spoke.

"You killed him. You killed him," she cried.

"Yes, and you're next," I spoke, as I threw down the axe and grabbed the shovel, trying to pick up the pieces and place them into the bottom of the

coffin. Picking up his head, I walked over to Robin and placed it on the porch beside her.

"What have you done?"

"I killed John."

"You're just sick," Robyn shouted, as she tried to get her hands out of the ropes.

"I'm not as sick as you and John. You two mutherfuckers are the sick ones, pumping your body with drugs, and on top of that, selling your child to have sex with a man for drugs. But I expected that when he told me that's how he got you in the first place. You all are sick and are going to die for it," I explained.

"You're not God, you know?" she shouted.

"I'm not him, but I was close to it," I stated, as I grabbed her chair and pulled her off the porch just like John. Her chair hit the ground and broke. She began squirming, trying to get out of the ropes. I just watched her.

Robin got out of the rope and tried to run on her heels. She looked so funny, as I laughed, walking behind her. As she got to the corner of the house, suddenly, a shovel went across her face. I stopped and began laughing. Uncle Earl had come to the rescue.

"I figured you needed some help." He laughed.

"I didn't but thanks. Grab her and bring her back here," I ordered. Uncle Earl grabbed her by her bloody feet and pulled her back to the backyard.

"You did a number on John. Shit," Uncle Earl called out.

"You should have been here to see it. Wait, how did you know they were here anyway?" I stopped, turning to look at him.

"I saw them pull in, and then, later, I saw you pulling the truck in. I figured something had gone down, so I eased on up here."

"Huh? Are you sure you're not watching my house?"

"That's what you pay me for, to watch your house, remember?" he replied.

"Yes, I do."

"Well, what do you want me to do with Robin?"

"I am going to throw her in that coffin and bury her alive."

"Before you do that, let me get some of that ass," he stated, as he began unbuckling his pants.

"You're sick," I stated, as I nodded my head, and he was down, spreading her legs.

"Aren't we all sick?" he stated, as he entered her and began humping away.

I walked off and went into the house. I didn't want to track blood and guts everywhere, so I limited myself to the kitchen. Getting the money off *the table, I began to hear Robin scream out. Walking back outside to the backyard with the money in my hand, Uncle Earl was punching Robin in the face, as she tried to fight back. After she stopped moving, he continued until he released. Getting up off her, he pulled up his pants then gave her a hard kick, as he buckled his black belt.*

"Are you finished playing?" I stated, as he looked up at me with this crazy look in his eyes.

"Yes, I finished. I always wanted to do that whore." He laughed.

Robin began moving around slowly and moaning.

"Here is 2,000 dollars. Help me put her in this coffin, so we can seal her up," I ordered. Uncle Earl grabbed the money quickly, shoving it into his pocket.

We picked up Robin and threw her into the coffin. Placing the lid over it, we nailed the coffin shut. As Uncle Earl drove the last nail into the coffin, Robin screamed.

"Shut up, old bitch," Uncle Earl yelled out, as he went around the coffin, hitting the top of it.

"I'm going to cut a hole in the top of it with her head. I want her to suffer for days until she dies," I stated, as I grabbed another tool and began sawing. After cutting a small hole in the coffin, I could see her face.

"Reagus, please, I don't want to die like this," she slowly spoke. For the first time in my life, I knew she was sincere. It kind of pulled at my heartstrings, but Uncle Earl brought me back to reality.

"Shut up, you old bitch. You're going to die, bitch," he called out. "Come on, Reagus, let's bury this bitch."

"You get that end." I pointed, as we picked up the heavy coffin and placed it over the shallow grave. We both let go, and it dropped down, settling in. Robyn's screams were echoing. You could tell that she was terrified. That was exactly how I wanted her to feel – just like I did in that mental institution.

Uncle Earl began throwing dirt on the shallow grave.

"Don't cover the hole, Uncle Earl," I stated.

"Okay," he replied, as he continued to put in more dirt.

After a few minutes, he had covered her, except for up by the head. Taking the shovel from him and packing the dirt down, I could see Robin's face, as I looked in the hole. She screamed and screamed for what seemed like hours.

"Where's John?" Uncle Earl asked.

"He's in the grave with Robin."

"I didn't see him."

"Well, let's just say he is a little chopped up." I laughed.

"You chopped him to pieces. Damn. You're a bad man," Uncle Earl replied, as he gave me a high five.

"Can you clean up all these tools and place them back in the barn?" I asked.

"You know I will."

I walked back inside the house, pulling my clothes off at the door. Grabbing a trash bag, I placed them in there and put the bag outside the back door.

Walking back to the bathroom, I took a long, hot shower. I felt kind of relieved, as the water hit my face, and steam filled the bathroom. After my shower, I put on clothes and headed out to see if Uncle Earl had finished cleaning up.

Stepping into the backyard, everything was cleaned neatly. He did a good job, but I saw he left John's head on the porch. I smiled at myself. Picking up the head, I went to the barn and grabbed a red rock crape tree. I buried John's head and planted my tree. I ended up burning the clothes in a barrel in the backyard. I could still hear Robin cry.

Three days had gone by, and I walked out to check on Robin every day. The first two days, she begged me to let her go. I just sat on the ground, talking to her about my day. On the third day, I came out, and she was dead. The stone look she had on her face told me she was dead. I looked closely because I thought I saw her move, and suddenly, a small black snake came out of her nose. I jumped back quickly. Getting the shovel, I placed it in the shallow grave and covered it up immediately.

After a week, I dug up the shallow grave and uncovered the dead bodies – Robin, John, and it looked like a family of black snakes were in there. They were all dead. I grabbed two red rock crape trees and walked out into the front yard. I buried Robin with the snakes under one and John under another. All the trees were blood red, but Robin's tree would bloom yellow roses, just like Raymond Dune.

CHAPTER 6

(Vindictive Valentine)

Dr. Amanda Smith asked, "When mutilating your victims' bodies, what made you want to give human eyes and blood to women as gifts on Valentine's Day?"

I replied, "No, I didn't stop to think about my actions. When I was in my zone, eating my favorite meat, I felt ten times stronger to dismember my prey. There was nothing to think about. I was hungry. Plus, I called Valentine's Day a vindictive day. Being angry with my mother, I began to hate all women at that time."

Occurred Incident: HAPPY VALENTINE'S DAY

Sitting at my desk at the shelter, I was thinking about Valentine's Day tomorrow. I was giving all the ladies gifts, chocolate covered cherries, a rose, and a bottle of my special wine. Startling me, the phone rang.

"Hello, Stewpot in Forest," I answered.

"Hello, Mr. Reagus. I wasn't sure if anyone was in the office or not, but I wanted to donate." This soft-spoken, seductive voice rose from the receiver.

"We are closed; I was just about to leave. How can I help you?"

"I wanted to donate to your organization. Is there any way I can do it today?" she spoke.

"As I stated before, I am about to leave," I replied, trying not to sound rude.

"I am outside of the Stewpot now. I had pulled into the parking lot, hoping that someone would still be there."

"Okay. I will come to the front door and let you in," I replied, hoping that she would just go away and come back another day.

Walking to the front door, I could see that she was a very gorgeous lady with long legs. Her hair was blonde and looked very clean. She was well built, but I could tell she was a little old, possibly my age.

"Hello again," I stated, as she stepped into the door, almost knocking me down. Her smell was immaculate, and I remembered it well. That smell belonged to Bonnie Logan.

"Hi, I'm Bonnie Logan," she stated with a huge smile on her face.

"I'm Reagus," I greeted, as I shook her hand. She pushed my hand down and gave me a huge hug, causing me to collapse.

"Oh, my God, are you alright?"

"I am okay. I just lost my balance," I faintly spoke, as I tried to catch my breath. Being unable to breathe, I continued. "Please, back up. I just need air."

"Of course," she whispered, as she backed up, giving me space.

"Can we do this tomorrow?" I managed to say, as I still lay on the floor, trying to get up.

"I can't possibly leave you like this," she spoke with concern.

"Trust me, I am okay."

"Well, you don't seem like it, Mr. Reagus," she replied, as she grabbed my arm, helping me get up off the floor. Her touch made me so weak, and the aroma coming from her body made me want to eat her.

"Please don't touch me, Ms. Logan," I softly spoke, as I took her hand off my arm.

"I'm so sorry, Mr. Reagus."

I walked off, making my way to my desk in the back. Putting my hands on the desk to guide me, I was barely moving. I could hear Ms. Logan's footsteps right behind me. Her presence was too much for me right now. I had to get myself together.

"Mr. Reagus, I will leave if you want me to," she continued, as I leaned against my desk and turned around to face her. She was right up on me. We stared at each other, eye to eye.

"You're acting as if you can't resist me," she surprisingly stated, as she stepped closer to me. I could feel her peppermint breath releasing under my nose.

"Maybe I can't resist you."

"Maybe," she slowly replied, as she softly touched my crotch and stroked my bone until it was fully erect.

"Why are you doing this to me?"

"I've had my eyes on you since Mary Alice told me about you. She bragged all the time about the famous Reagus. The man whom she couldn't live without."

"How do you know Mary Alice?"

"Don't worry about that. Take me," Bonnie ordered, as she grabbed both my hands and placed them under her dress. Touching her sweetness, I guided my hand a little farther, feeling her wetness. She was very wet and inviting.

Lifting her legs, I entered her with one finger. Soft moans escaped her mouth, as she unbuckled my pants. Pulling down my pants and boxers, she began stroking me. Almost throwing up on her, I tried to push her away. Falling to her knees, she took me into her mouth. With my hands over my mouth, I tried not to throw up on her. Putting Bonnie onto the desk, she smiled at me. Standing up to face me, Bonnie leaned against me and kissed me. I kissed her back passionately. Things were so hot and steamy that I almost fainted again.

"Why me?" I mumbled.

"Why not you?" she whispered.

As we continued to kiss, I placed Bonnie on my desk, opening her legs. Grabbing my manhood, I entered her without a condom. Rushing inside her, I ached for her. I yearned for her love. I nibbled on her face and neck, trying to fight the urge to kill her. I wanted so much to taste her meat again. Instead, I pulled out of her wetness and began performing oral. It tasted even better than I would have imagined. Bonnie screamed, as she reached her peak. Standing tall, I re-entered her and pounded away, stroking and stroking Bonnie until I reached my peak.

Laying Bonnie on the floor, we stroked at each other until we both collapsed. My urge to eat her went away at that moment. I lay there, taking in her smell. I kept nibbling on Bonnie, trying to eat her, but I could not. My body wanted more of Bonnie Logan. Could she be the same Bonnie Logan from Sebastopol, Mississippi?

VALENTINE'S DAY

As I got my chocolate-covered cherries ready for the ladies, Uncle Earl helped me get them out of the freezer at the shelter. They were homemade chocolate-covered eyeballs – human eyeballs. For each victim I killed, I removed their eyeballs carefully and placed them in jars of water until ready for use. Preparing for Valentine's Day, I removed my eyes from the water. After poking a needle in them and removing the fluid content, I got another needle and then inserted them with chocolate. Afterward, I dipped them in chocolate. Some I placed with nuts on them, and others, I did not. Everything looked delicious.

After I prepared my chocolate-covered eyes, I opened at least fifty bottles of that cheap wine, pouring wine mixed with blood. Mixing blood and wine, I developed my favorite drink. I had to seal the wine top back. It took some time to search the YouTube videos. I bought the materials and the machine, but sealing those new wine bottles was done professionally. I came up with a fake company name. The ladies were going to love my special gifts, and everyone received three roses as well. I was going to be the talk of the town.

I gave gifts from 9 am to 12 pm.

"I've never seen so many pretty women before," Uncle Earl gawked, as he handed me bottles and bottles of wine to give away.

"Me either, but I like it," I remarked.

"I do too," he replied as if he was lusting.

"Clean the slob from your mouth, Uncle Earl. You don't want these women to call us perverts." I laughed.

"Hey, Mr. Reagus," a woman from my old apartment complex spoke. She was about seventy years old.

"Hey, Ms. Pearline, how are you doing?"

"I'm wonderful, baby. This is a nice thing that you are doing. Running the homeless shelter is very good as well. You are a kind young man," Ms. Pearline remarked.

"Thank you, Ms. Pearline. Now, you enjoy those chocolate-covered cherries."

"I need a bottle or two of that wine as well." She laughed.

"You can have two bottles." I laughed, as Uncle Earl handed her two bottles.

Ms. Pearline walked away with a big smile on her face. Other ladies watched, as I smiled at her until she disappeared.

"Mr. Reagus, do you want me as your girlfriend?" another lady asked, as I turned around, and this short, African American lady stood. She was about 5'5" and weighed around two hundred and eighty pounds.

"I'm not interested in having a girlfriend right now," I replied.

"You must be gay," she smarted off.

"Why do I have to be gay?"

"You don't want no woman."

"I said I didn't want no girlfriend," I replied.

"Yeah, you are gay," she stated, as she snatched the box of chocolate covered eyes and rose out of my hand. She continued, "Give me my bottle of wine, Earl. Ain't it free?"

"I shouldn't give you anything since you are being rude and shit. Reagus doesn't have to give you nothing," Uncle Earl shouted.

"Give me my wine, Earl," she yelled out, causing the other women to stare. I nodded my head for him to give it to her.

"Get out of here, you old bitch," Uncle Earl whispered. I let out a small giggle, as she snatched the bottle of wine from Uncle Earl and walked off.

"With your rude ass," Uncle Earl smarted off.

"Uncle Earl, don't be so mean. Today is Valentine's Day," I replied.

We smiled at each other and finished giving out gifts to everyone. As soon as noon came around, we wrapped up. After finishing up my day at the shelter, I went home. Suddenly, my cell phone rang. Unknown caller.

"Hello," I spoke softly.

"Hello, Mr. Reagus," that soft, seductive voice whispered.

"How did you get my number?"

"I've had your number, just never used it. Remember, Mary Alice was a good friend of mine."

"You keep telling me." I laughed. "How can I help you, Ms. Logan?" I asked.

"I want to come in and join you," she invited.

"Come in where?"

"Don't be silly. You know I'm here."

"So, you're outside?" I asked.

"Yes, I'm outside at this silly black gate. Come get me," she ordered.

"Yes, ma'am." I laughed, as I rushed down to get Bonnie.

As soon as I let her in, I took her right there at my black gate. Her smell filled the air, as I stroked her. To my surprise, after that night, Bonnie stayed with me for an entire week. My body craved her over and over.

As Bonnie slept, I devoured my favorite meat every day. Cooking for her was strange, but I did it just for her to stay around. I was feeling drunk in love with her meat. After a week, she was gone. I craved fresh meat, and the hunt was on for more.

I must say that I wasn't interested in eating the feet, hands, and head of the body. Odd but true. I always cut them off and tossed them under my red rock crape trees. I ordered so many of the red rock crape trees from Lowe's and Home Depot. I ordered over fifty hundred trees altogether. A yellow and red rose bush was ordered. They were for the family members I planned to kill. The head was big and didn't have any meat after I took the brain out and ate it. I wasn't into the hair, but the eyes were made for my guests. My women had them, as I made them into chocolate-covered eyes. They thought they were chocolate-covered cherries. I

****

Dr. Amanda Smith asked, "My understanding is you tortured four women at your home. What happened?"

"You seem very anxious to know exactly what happened," I stated.

I continued. "Well, first, there was Sarah. She was a Black female with a nappy mohawk on her head. I knew she was going to die when she first pulled up at the house. When she got out, she was big and fat. I didn't remember her that way. She was a cute girl, but things changed. That bitch had to die, deceiving me."

"People change."

"Yes, and change got her killed. Now, my second victim is Tina. Slender girl, short, straight hair. After I drugged her and stripped down her clothes, she had to die. My third victim was my most hated victim. Her name was Erin. She always gave me hell in college. I invited her just to torture her. And the fourth girl was Vickie. My favorite girl." I smiled.

I continued, "I picked these girls out because they tortured me in college. They made fun of me and talked about me like I was nothing. I wasn't sure if they would accept my invitation to dinner, but all four did. I decided to kill them, eat them. If they hadn't come to the house, then I would have made plans to kidnap them. That would have been harder, but the cunts made it very easy."

"Why call them cunts?" Dr. Amanda Smith asked.

"They're cunts just like you. As I was saying, I was surprised they all showed up, especially Erin. She made me sick to my stomach. Her murder was going to be violent."

Occurred Incident: *TASTY CHOICE*

I stood on the porch, pacing, waiting for my four guests to show up. I'd been planning this for months. I had to research where these four girls lived and so on. I knew them all from college.

Suddenly, I saw a black Chevy Malibu creep up the driveway. It was the pathetic little girl, Erin. As she drove up, I began waving like we hadn't seen each other in years. Which was true, we hadn't seen each other in years. Then, she turned off the car and exited.

"What's this about, Reagus?" she asked, as she approached the end of the steps.

"I'm having a surprise Valentine's treat for people I liked in college," I made up, as I reached out with my hand, but she knocked it down.

"Sure, you did. It seems like it's more to it than that," she spoke.

"That's it."

"Am I the only one showing up to this so-called dinner?" she asked, as she eased up the steps.

Erin was an Asian female with short hair and a slim body. I never noticed the stretch marks she had on her arms. I guess that happened over the years. The smell of her skin made me sick to my stomach. I wanted to turn her around, but I continued with her because I needed to finish what I planned to do.

"There are three more people," I stated, as another car came up the driveway, then another, then another.

I continued. "There are my other three guests."

"Let me guess. You hadn't seen them in years either," Erin asked, as she approached me. I stepped backward because the smell was sickening.

"You're correct."

"Hello," Sarah yelled out, as she exited her vehicle.

"Hello to you," I responded, as I stepped away from Erin to go meet her. Sarah was a dark-skinned, Black female with a mohawk haircut, short and nappy, fat with hips.

Tina and Vickie exited their vehicles.

"Hey, Reagus," Tina softly spoke. She was a Black, slender, thin, anorexic-looking female with short, brunette hair as well. Her arms had sores all over them. Another sickening project, I thought.

"Hello, Reagus," Vickie spoke, as she approached me. She was a thicker white female with a big butt. My first time seeing a white girl with so much ass.

"Everybody come into my home. I will let everyone know what this is about before you all ask. I know you all are wondering what this is about," I yelled out, so everyone could hear.

Erin took it upon herself to enter without waiting for me.

"You look good, Reagus," Sarah stated, as she walked up to me.

"You've been working out, I see," Vickie said, as she grabbed my arm, interlocking us together. Tina walked slowly behind.

We entered my home, and everyone looked surprised. Eyebrows were raised, as they entered the foyer.

"This is a lovely home," Vickie stated, as they all looked around.

"Come into the kitchen," I said, as I led them that way. Someone smelled so good, but I couldn't tell because they all were grouped, except for Erin. Once we entered the kitchen, she was already seated.

"Nice setup, Reagus. I still want to know what this is about," Erin said.

"Everyone, please take a seat," I requested, as I took a seat at the head. *"Is everything okay with you, Tina? I noticed you have been quiet since you got here,"* I continued.

"I'm fine, Reagus. I think I ate something, and it didn't sit well with me," Tina said, as she took a seat.

"I'm sorry to hear that," I replied.

"Get on with it, Reagus," Erin rushed as if she had somewhere to go.

"If you need to leave, you may do so. I don't want to keep you here. It seems like you have somewhere to be," I stated to her.

"Just curious, nowhere to go," she replied.

"Okay, ladies, I know it's after Valentine's Day, but I wanted you all to feel extra special. I put a dinner together for you all. I know this is out of the normal for me, but I wanted you to know I appreciate everything you all have taught me," I spoke to everyone.

"It is out of the ordinary," Vickie said.

"I was surprised to hear from you," Tina stated. She continued. *"How did you know where I lived?"*

"You're correct, but three of you attended college with me at East Central. Tina, you're the only one from elementary school. But I learned

*where you stay from your brother, Trey," I
answered back.*

*"He's always telling people where I'm at,"
Tina replied.*

*"I know I have had bad experiences with
you all, but I wanted to show you how much you
have taught me," I spoke, as I grabbed the wine and
poured drinks.*

*"Yes, we did have bad experiences, so why
invite me?" Erin called out.*

*"Yes, Erin, you picked at me every single
day of my college years. There wasn't a day that
went by without you shitting on me," I replied. My
hands were about to start shaking, but I had to
control them. I wanted to kill her right then and
there but not yet.*

"It wasn't that bad," she remarked.

*"Erin, it wasn't bad for you, but it was
terrible for me. I found out that what you were
doing was bullying. I cried every day and didn't
want to go to school because of you. I tried to take
my life a couple of times. You just didn't know how
you made me feel," I remarked, as I stared at her.*

*"Well, our experience together wasn't too
bad. Was it, Reagus?" Vickie asked, as she lifted
the wine glass to her mouth.*

*"Vickie, you were just as bad as Erin. I
guess Erin took over from there. Once you were in*

my shoes and they picked on you, you were with me, an outsider," I added.

"I apologize for what I did, and yes, I did get picked on," Vickie said.

"I forgave you years ago when I saw my psychiatrist. I held a grudge against you for a long time, but as I said, I learned to forgive."

"What about me, Reagus?" Tina asked.

"You did nothing, Tina. I just didn't like you from the beginning. I saw how you bullied my friends. You were a little like Erin, but less crazy. Erin put her hands on people. Fighting them." I continued, "The wine is delicious, taste it."

"How do we know you're not trying to kill us?" Sarah asked.

"If you believed that, you wouldn't be here."

"I didn't know what it was about, but now that I know all of us bullied you, I am thinking about leaving," Sarah stated.

"Girl, sit down. Ain't nobody trying to kill you. They should because you sure is ugly," Erin called out.

"You bitch," Sarah replied, as she stood up.

"Ladies, there will be no fighting in my home. Just drink your wine and unwind. Dinner will be out soon."

"Good because I'm hungry," Vickie mentioned.

*"Tina, are you sure you're okay?" I asked
again.*

*"I don't know if it was the food my mama
cooked or the wine you put out," she replied,
holding her stomach.*

*"Do you need to go to the restroom?" I
politely asked.*

"Yes, please."

"It's down the hall to the right."

*"Thank you," she replied, as she got up and
walked away.*

*I was happy to know that at least one of
them drank my special wine. I had a little human
blood and a few berries from the belladonna plant.
One was about to go down. Now, I could get the
rest of them to drink up.*

*"Where's the food, Reagus?" Erin spoke, as
she picked up a fork.*

"I will go and get it."

*"Hurry up, I have other stuff to do than to
be entertained by you."*

*"The wine did nothing to me," Sarah spoke,
as she picked up her wine glass to drink more.*

*"There is nothing wrong with the wine. That
girl is probably pregnant," Vickie spoke.*

*Finally, I made it back with steaks, potatoes,
and broccoli. I took my time and placed food on
everyone's plate. Erin didn't wait for grace; she
just went for it. She ate like a fucking pig. Vickie*

and Sarah dug in. Tina hadn't made it back yet, so I
went to check on her.

"Tina, are you okay?" I asked, as I knocked
on the bathroom door. There was no answer.

"Tina, are you okay?" I asked again, as I
turned the doorknob. Opening the door, she lay out
on the floor. I closed the door back and headed
back to the table.

"What's wrong with that girl?" Erin asked
between chews.

"She was throwing up, so I let her be," I
replied, as I sat down to feast.

"I will check on her," Vickie volunteered, as
she stood up.

"She'll be just fine. Sit down and enjoy your
meal," I demanded before I knew it.

"Well, yes, sir, I sure will," Vickie said and
sat back down to eat.

We all sat there in silence for once, enjoying
our food. Sarah was smacking like a pig. I hated
that. I was checking out everyone's skin. Tina had
on a summer dress with body sores everywhere.
Black spots all over. I could hardly stand it. Vickie
had on a nice shirt with nice skin. And that Erin had
on a white wife beater. She seemed so boyish. I
hated that for her because she would be the one I
killed first. She seemed tougher than the rest of
them.

"So, Reagus, how did you get this house?" Erin asked.

"My grandparents died and left me this lovely home. Do you like it?"

"Too much for me. Too fancy."

"I'm feeling sick," Vickie interrupted. She vomited on her plate.

"Oh, shit," Sarah yelled out, as she jumped up. She was sitting next to Vickie. "Dammit, girl, you almost got me," Sarah stated, as she fell backward.

"What the fuck is going on? What's wrong with them?" Erin said, as she jumped up and fell back in her chair. Her head rested on the back of the chair, and her eyes rolled into the back of her head. Vickie's face fell into her vomit on the plate.

"Well, ladies, it's time." I laughed, as I sat up and smiled. Clapping my hands, I walked around, picking up everyone's plate and cleaning the table. My belladonna plants began to work.

"Damn, I didn't think you ladies would ever go down," I spoke to them, as they laid out everywhere. Clearing the table, I placed Erin on top of it and tied her down. The table was bolted to the floor; it was not moving. I tied Vickie and Sarah to the chairs.

I sat there for a long time, waiting for Erin to wake. I wanted her to be alive and screaming when I killed her. I wanted her to look directly into my face.

"About time you got your boyish ass up. It took long enough," I said, as she moved around, trying to move her arms.

"You better let me up from here, Reagus," she demanded.

"And what if I don't? You're going to hurt me? Let's get real. The only way you're getting off this table is when you die. And then, I would have to carry you."

"Reagus, I promise I won't tell anyone," she stated, as she looked around at Vickie and Sarah. She continued, "What have you done to everyone?"

"Your mind should be on saving you and only you."

"Please don't hurt me," she begged.

I paid her no mind. I gathered my baseball bat. When I jumped up on the table, Erin began to whimper. "Please, Reagus, don't hurt me."

"This will only hurt you if you let it get to you," I replied, as I lifted the bat to hit her.

"Reagus, no," she screamed.

"Too late." I laughed, as I hit her on the top of the head with the bat. Then again, then again. "Well, damn, I hope I didn't kill you." I laughed again, as Erin was out cold or dead. Checking her pulse, I was relieved. I didn't mean to hit her that hard. I needed her to be alive.

"What are you doing?" a soft voice spoke, as I stood.

I looked around, and it was Tina. That bitch finally woke up at the wrong time. I needed her to sleep, while I killed the others.

"Don't you worry about them." I laughed, as I jumped down off the table and wrapped my arms around her. She began yelling. Little girl with a big voice.

"Shut up, you fucking cunt. Nobody is going to hear you," I said, as I wrapped my fingers around her neck and squeezed. Tina passed out right there on the floor. Laughing, I turned back to Erin. Jumping on the table, I began slapping her over and over until she woke up. Barely awake at that.

"I wish you stop passing out on me. What is your problem?"

"Please help me," Erin faintly spoke.

"The only help you are getting tonight is death. Death by bleeding to death, maybe."

"Why are you..."

"Don't ask me why! We all just talked at the table about you bullying me. You admitted that you did it. That's why I am going to torture you."

"I apologize. I apologize for what I've done," she whimpered.

"It's not going to work. If you apologized as Vickie did, you probably wouldn't be in this

situation right now. But, then again, I've been waiting for a long time to kill you off. It would disappoint me if I let you go. Anyway, on with the next."

I walked into the kitchen and grabbed a saw and a knife. I wanted her to suffer.

"I found the tools I needed. Now, I just must fix you up."

"Please, Reagus."

"Please, Reagus," I repeated. I continued, "You didn't say that when you bullied me as you did, so don't fucking beg me now."

"I have kids."

"No, you don't. I have researched everything about you, and there are no kids. Just you and that old-ass dog you have. You work twelve-hour shifts, you barely visit your family, and you have no real friends. So, don't try to trick me."

"Reagus."

I paid no attention to her. Taking off her shoes, I smelled her feet.

"Your feet smell just like your apartment, like a dog. You needed to clean up that shit that reaps out your door."

"You can't do this to me."

"Yes, I can, and I am."

I held her ankle and began to saw. Tina moved around, moaning; I kicked her in the head and sent her back to sleep. Erin screamed. It was music to my ears. I saw the other ankle disconnecting from the body. Both feet lay on the ground in from of me. She cried and screamed like no other.

I started again at her knees and took them both clean from her body. She was still screaming like an idiot. I figured she would die by now, but she didn't. She was screaming though. That didn't bother me.

Stopping, I got some rope and tied Tina down. I was enjoying myself with Erin, and I forgot she was loose. Laughing out loud, I kicked Tina in the back of the head over and over. The pounding of her head caused a few cuts on her face.

"Leave her alone," Erin cried.

"There you go again, worrying about the wrong thing."

"I can't save myself, so I tried to save someone," she cried again.

"Shut the fuck up."

I grabbed the knife, cutting into her eyes. Pulling out eyeballs, I laughed and ate them both. Erin was dead by then. I grabbed the saw again and cut out her heart. I ate it too because she was a mean little bastard. She deserved to die.

"Help! Help me!" Sarah yelled over and over. I turned around to look at her and laughed. Tears were falling down her face, and I approached her.

"Do you think anyone can hear you?" I asked, as she continued to scream.

"You're sick," she screamed in my face.

"Okay, I'll take that," I replied calmly.

I threw the saw on the ground and picked up the knife again. I licked the blood off the knife, nicking my tongue. "Dammit, Reagus Dune, you sick fuck," I yelled at myself, as Sarah's eyes got big, while I walked toward her.

"Stay away from me, kill her," she yelled out.

"Well, seems like I'm not the only one who is sick."

"I'm not sick."

"Then why tell me to kill her?"

"Maybe you will let me go. I promise…"

"Don't say you promise not to tell. Not that bullshit."

"Reagus, we can kill together, just let me go," Sarah spoke.

I rushed her, beating her face in with the butt end of the knife. Her nose was busted open with blood and snot hanging. Looking at the sores on her arms, I began stabbing her arms over and over. She screamed like a newborn baby. The knife kept getting stuck; it had me frustrated. As I stabbed her over and over with them ugly ass sores all over her, Vickie began to wake up and so did Tina. Tina was squirming, trying to get loose, and Vickie started that damn screaming too.

I decapitated Sarah's head from her body. Blood shot up in my face. Vickie's chair fell over. She was trying to kick, but I had her tied down well. Cleaning my face, I walked into the kitchen. As soon as I stepped out, Tina was gone. Her rope came loose.

Picking up the knife, I walked around the front door to sniff her out. Suddenly, she hit me on the head with a lamp. I was dazed. Instead of her rescuing herself, she went over to free Vickie. I gathered myself and threw the knife directly into her temple. She fell over like a rock. Rubbing my head, I went over to make sure she was dead. She moaned, so I kicked the knife deeper into her temple. I knew that bitch was dead.

"See what you did? I was going to let her live," I lied.

"You planned to kill us from the beginning."

"Of course, I plotted on you all. If you hadn't of came, then the wine I sent would have killed you. I wanted to make sure the job was done. I know eventually, I will get caught one day, but not today. Well, let's get this date started, I have so much to do. Look at all their bodies," I spoke.

Suddenly, a knock came at the door. Vickie began to scream. I grabbed her mouth as fast as I could. The person tried to open the front door. I

*heard the knob ring. Whomever it was left. Then,
there was a knock at the back door. I could see
someone trying to look in. My back door was
unlocked. I would have to kill whomever it was.
Damn, what the fuck? This was not supposed to
happen. Suddenly, the back door opened. My heart
was beating so fast. Peeping around the corner was
Uncle Earl.*

*"Dammit, Uncle Earl. You scared the hell
out of me," I spoke, as I let go of Vickie, and she
began screaming for help.*

*"What the hell are you doing in here? I saw
all those cars in the yard and thought you were
having a party without me," he stated.*

*"It was a party, but it's over. We had drinks,
and I enjoyed them as you see." I laughed.*

"I see you did."

"You're fucking sick too," Vickie yelled.

*"Go and get some barbed wire. I need to
shut her mouth," I instructed Uncle Earl.*

*"Okay. You should let me play with her first
then kill her. It's been a while."*

*"Okay, she might need a good dick." We
laughed.*

"Hell yeah." Uncle Earl smiled.

*"You keep him away from me, Reagus. I will
do anything you ask me to," Vickie stated.*

*"You're going to do anything I want
anyway," I said, as Uncle Earl and I untied her*

from the chair. She fought us, but Uncle Earl got her down. We tied her up with her hands behind her back. I walked out. Uncle Earl raped Vickie repeatedly for about a few minutes.

"Are you done having fun?" I asked, as I walked back into the kitchen. Uncle Earl was standing over Vickie with his clothes pulled up.

"What happened?" I continued to ask, as Uncle Earl was looking lost, pale faced.

"I don't know what happened. She was coming out of the ropes, so I hit her head over and over, then she stopped moving. I just stood here, kicking her, to see if she moved," he explained.

"Dammit, Uncle Earl, I wanted to kill her. You took my joy away from me but oh well," I stated, as I motioned for him to help me clean up.

"Help me clean this mess up," I ordered.

We began cleaning up the mess and burning the bodies under the red crape trees I planted out in the field in the backyard. They were there to help my plants grow faster. Good fertilizer.

CHAPTER 7

(4th of July Block Party)

Dr. Amanda Smith asked, "What was the purpose of serving human meat at a block party you hosted?"

"I shared because I had so much that I needed to make room for more meat. There was more than enough. The neighborhood didn't care as long as it was free. So, I served them a free meal. Many came back for more and brought friends. I had the whole neighborhood loving me for my good deed," I replied.

Occurred Incident: HAPPY 4TH OF JULY

"Have you prepared all the meat we are serving today?" I asked Uncle Earl, as he gathered coolers and coolers of meat on ice.

"Everything is ready. We have twenty pans of potato salad, twenty pans of bacon beans, drinks, and water," he replied.

"What about my favorite wine? Are those bottles secured in the van?"

"Why are you serving wine to these fools? They are only coming for free food. Liquor will only make them crazy."

"True. But the wine is for those that donate $50.00 or more to the homeless shelter," I stated, as I helped carry the big coolers of meat to the van.

"I understand what you're doing now. You must have a lot of money to do all this. But you do know you're opening a new can of worms," Uncle Earl remarked, as he stopped and stared at me.

"What do you mean?"

"You are serving free food to these fools; they are going to be at your door regularly, trying to get something free. Believe me, I know the neighborhood."

"Well, to my understanding, these are all our relatives. You don't want to feed your people?"

"Of course, I do. I just don't want you to be taken advantage of. You take care of me, so I am here to take care of you," Uncle Earl explained.

"It's all good, Uncle Earl. I'm a big boy, and I believe that I can take care of myself. I'm not worried about them bugging me. I have a plan."

"What plan?"

"If they do bug me, I will give them the Robin and John treatment. Do you know what I mean?"

"Most definitely, I do. And I will be standing right there to help you. Trust me, these people are plotting too."

"Plotting about what?"

"They're jealous of the stuff you're doing, and they want in. I'm surprised nobody has broken into your house yet. These people don't care; they are looking out for themselves."

"Well, Uncle Earl, I am not worried about them breaking into my house. We're out in the country. Everybody knows everybody's business. And I am sure if I issued a reward, somebody would rat them out."

"You're right about that."

Silence approached us, as we continued to gather things into two vans and drive just a short distance down this dirt road. We had a nice setup. Two of the cooks from the homeless shelter were standing over the barbecue grills, cooking. A few of the ladies from the shelter had set up tables for the bacon beans and potato salad. I had a van with a person standing by with wine. There were one hundred bottles of wine.

"This is a different kind of meat," Chief Charles stated. He was a short, bald, Black guy with a few extra pounds.

"Yes, it is. It's my favorite kind of meat. You'll love it," I stated.

"I've tasted it, and it is delicious. I can't stop eating," he joked.

"I understand how good it is, but you have to share with these many guests we have coming."

"You mean the mob we have coming. People from different areas are coming, not only the ones in the neighborhoods."

"That's a good thing. I am hoping the people bring their appetites because we have plenty."

"I hear you. You are too kind, Mr. Reagus," Chief Charles stated, as he looked over at Chief Beamon who was slaying away. Chief Beamon was a tall, slim, white man. He was quiet and always kept to himself.

"Thank you, Chief Charles. Just trying to share with the neighborhood and make everyone happy. Hopefully, they will donate by buying this wine to help with the shelter," I remarked.

I knew if they had one taste, they would be craving more. I was serving Bibi Graetz Casamatte. This wine was made from Sangiovese. Graetz's entry-level red was a super value with lush, energetic plum and cherry flavors. It was a very cheap wine, but I made it sound expensive. Opening all the bottles and mixing human blood, they wouldn't know the difference. Once they got a taste of that human blood, they would crave more. That was why I put a small shot size sample out for the people. Somebody was going to splurge and buy it. The more who tasted the human blood, the better.

After setting everything up and the meat was ready, the servers I hired began fixing plates. So *many cars started coming in, wanting food. Luckily, I did have both chefs come in early that morning and start cooking. Those baked beans were made with cooked hamburger meat and a cup of human blood. I had to strain the blood, making sure there were no bone fragments from my violent kills. The bodies with damaged skin, I skinned and cut the meat to pieces just for the 4th of July Block Party. Having them hanging upside down and draining their blood took time and patience.*

The potato salad was the only thing untainted. It was purely old-fashioned, southern style from Vowell's grocery store. I wanted to mix something special with it but decided not to. I was already serving my favorite meat with barbecue sauce, my special beans with human blood, and my famous wine with human blood. These people were about to get a taste of what I had been craving. Uncle Earl just didn't know that I fattened the hogs for the kill.

"Why do you have a mask on?" this woman asked, as she approached me with a big plate overstocked with food.

"It's nothing serious. It's the smoke from the barbecue grills," I replied, hoping she would move on.

"Oh, okay. Do you have a girlfriend?"
"No, why?"

"I was just wondering because you are kind of cute."

"Well, thank you, young lady," I stated, as I tried to walk away, and she grabbed my arm. I snatched away quickly, and she jumped.

"I'm sorry. You took me by surprise by grabbing me," I remarked. Truth was that I hated to be touched. I didn't want anyone's dirty hands on me.

"I didn't mean to scare you. I just wanted to say that if you need anything, I mean anything, just let me know," she offered, as she opened her blouse a little to expose her breasts.

"Thank you. I sure will," I replied, as I walked off. I wasn't messing with that ugly girl. She had needle marks all over her arms. Her body had sores all over it. But I did make a mental note to kill her. There was no doubt in my mind that she was going to die. That bitch had to die for touching me.

"Hey there, boy," this elderly man yelled out.

"Hey." I waved and went over to Chef Charles. I figured the old man would follow. He looked like he had something to say.

"Say there, boy, you give away a lot of meat," he remarked.

"Yes, sir, we are feeding the neighborhood. Would you like a plate?" I offered.

This man was very skinny with a dark complexion. His eyes were brown with a green rim around them. Unique.

"I see you're serving all this free meat. It must be human meat. You know there are people out here in the world eating people. I have tasted a few myself, and that's what it tastes like," he stated, hoping to get a reaction out of me.

"So, you eat people?" Chef Charles asked, as he flipped over a few pieces of meat.

"I have eaten a few. I know meat, and this is it," he admitted.

"Well, you need to get your human-eating ass from over here. These aren't the humans we are serving. So, go on with your bull," Chef Charles spoke out.

"Why do you think it's human? Just because you have eaten a few people doesn't make it what you say," I interrupted.

"Boy, don't tell me lies. You have people eating other people around here. But I'll keep your secret." He laughed, as he gave me a light punch on my arm.

"I think it's time for you to go, old man. Don't want you scaring people around here."

Suddenly, he began yelling, "Y'all fools eating people. They are serving y'all human meat."

"Get out of here, old man," Chef Charles yelled out.

"Father, no," a woman called out, as she approached the old man.

"Is this your father?" I asked.

"Yes, he is. He is a very sick man. I'm sorry that he is bothering you," she remarked, as she grabbed him by the hand and walked off.

"Y'all eating human meat. Y'all going to rot in hell," he shouted, as he walked away. The lady grabbed two big plates that she had placed on her car. She even purchased four bottles of wine.

After she placed her father on the passenger side of the car, she handed him his plate. He kept staring at me, as he took a big bite out of the barbecue meat. We continued to stare at each other for a few minutes until his daughter got out of the car and approached me.

"I'm sorry, sir, but my father would like another plate with just meat." She shied away. Her smile was bright with white teeth.

"Yes, ma'am, he can have as many plates as he wants," I stated, as I directed one of the helpers to give him two plates of just meat.

"Thank you so much, Mister," she spoke.

"You're welcome."

The lady walked off with the two plates and got into her car. I could still see the old man staring at me with those unique eyes. He was eating the meat like he was starving to death. I was glad that

*he was leaving because these people around here
might believe him.*

*As the day ended after serving everyone, we
were completely wiped out. The wine also sold out
in two hours. After cleaning up, we all headed
home. That night after my shower, I couldn't help
but think about that old man. His face, his eyes, and
the words he spoke stuck in my head. I found out
later his name was Bud Logan. Reminded me so
much of Bonnie Logan. She was the first girl who
gave me my first taste of human flesh.*

****

Dr. Amanda Smith asked, "Was there
anyone you killed who you will always remember:
an unforgettable crime?"

"It's funny that you ask that. There was an
unforgettable kill that devastated me. Every time I
close my eyes, I can see it playing over and over.
That's how I got caught. After my kill, Uncle Earl
came to check on me and saw I was devastated. I
am the one who told him to call the police and
report me. I wanted to die," I replied.

Occurred Incident: DISPOSAL OF BODY PARTS

*"Hey, Reagus, do you want to come to our
Skittles' party?" Todd asked. He was a boy I met in
my accounting class. He was nerdy but cool.*

177

"What's a Skittles' party?

"Reagus, you have to get out more often."

"Where is this party going to be?" I asked, excited because he asked.

"It will be in Scott Hall, Room 214."

"What do I need to bring?"

"Just bring yourself since it's your first time."

"Cool. Thanks."

"Don't be late," Todd shouted, as he rushed off to another class.

I immediately took out my phone and put in, "what is a Skittles' party?" Todd made me feel kind of dumb. I should have known what a Skittles' party was. As I researched on my phone, it pulled up that a Skittles' party could take the form of a home filled with teenagers where everyone brought all the prescription medications they had on hand and pooled them. You mixed all the drugs and consume them by the handful. Continuing reading, it said that the deadly side effects of this were a sharp rise in blood pressure and heart rate levels. Also, seizures or hallucinations. The prescription drugs mixed like that could have you become drowsy, or it could have others extremely fidgety and excited.

I was thinking to myself that these kids were nuts, but then again, so was I. I had never been invited to any kind of party before nor had I ever used drugs, but it seemed like it would be very exciting.

Later that night around ten, I showed up at Todd's room in Scott Hall. I debated whether to come or not. But Todd was convincing, blowing up my phone like he was my woman.

"You made it. Come on in and make yourself at home." Todd invited me in, as he patted me on the back.

"I researched this Skittles' party after you made me feel stupid." I laughed.

"A lot of people don't know what it is. We don't go around telling everybody about our little party," he explained.

"Right," I responded, as I looked around the room. There were about three girls and four of us boys.

"Everybody, Reagus is here," Todd shouted, as I walked into the room, and he opened the door for another girl I knew from my accounting class.

"I got the drugs," Denise shouted, as she patted me on the back and ran to the middle of the floor, holding a bag of pills.

"I got the cough syrup," another girl, Sonya, yelled out.

"Y'all drugs are weak. I have Percocet this time." Josh smiled, as he pulled the small bags of pills from his coat.

"I have something even better than that."
Denise laughed. "I have Xanax."

They all started laughing, and Todd pulled out this big, glass bowl. Josh pulled a small red and white cooler from the side of his bed. That cooler contained many different bottles of alcohol such as Peach Cîroc, Jack Daniels, and a bottle called 1800.

Todd pulled up a table, mixing all the pills. Sonya and Denise kept pulling out packs of Robitussin PM and Sudafed. After they were done, the bowl was very colorful like Skittles. I understood why they called it a Skittles' party.

After Todd mixed them, he turned on the television. The girls started taking off their clothes. I took a deep breath.

"Don't be scared, Reagus. These girls won't bite you," Todd called out, as he took off his shirt.

"I'm not afraid." I laughed.

They all grabbed handfuls of pills and downed them quickly, chasing with a shot of liquor. So, I grabbed a small handful and took them as well with a shot.

After what seemed like hours, I took off my clothes, and Sonya crawled over to me, performing oral sex on me. By this time, the room was a full-blown orgy. The music was blasting, and I was feeling wonderful. My mind kept going back to the side effect of seizures and shit. After a while, I forgot all about it.

Glancing at my phone, after I managed to get it out of my pocket, it read 3:15 a.m. The time had gone by so quickly. Everyone in the entire room was asleep except for Todd and Denise. They were going at it like dogs.

I stood on my feet and fell backwards. Getting up again, I tried to get control of myself to leave. I had to go home. Struggling to put on my clothes after about fifteen minutes, I was fully dressed.

"Where are you going?" Todd asked, as Denise kept performing oral sex on him. She was sucking so hard, like a vacuum cleaner.

"Man, I have to get home," I slowly stated, as I glanced at my phone again.

"You should stay here and sleep those pills off. I don't want to be responsible if you get out there and kill yourself or shit, kill somebody else," he responded.

"I'm not going to kill nobody. I got this," I replied, as I moved slowly to the door.

"Let him go. He is grown," Denise slurred, as she continued oral on Todd.

"I'll see you at class tomorrow," I told Todd.

"Tomorrow is Saturday. There is no class tomorrow."

"Oh, yeah, my bad." I laughed, as I opened the door and disappeared into the night.

Getting into my car, I must have passed out. The next thing I knew, my doorbell at the house was ringing. It kept going off, and then, my door opened. It sounded like I heard a baby. As I sat very still on the couch, Joyce rounded the corner, carrying our baby, Brady.

"What the hell is going on here, Reagus?" she shouted. Her voice sounded like a shotgun going off in my ear.

"What do you mean?" I slurred.

"Why are you sitting on the couch, naked? Your black gate is wide open with your truck still running, and your front door is wide open," she shouted.

"I don't know. Somebody must have broken in," I slurred again, as I tried to get up but fell over.

Joyce put baby Brady down on the couch and rushed over, trying to help me up. Pushing her off, I struggled and stood on my own.

"Look at yourself. What happened?" She pointed at my groin area.

"What?"

I looked down at my groin area, and my cock was glued to my leg with white stuff all around it.

*"Don't know what happened there either." I
laughed and grabbed her.*

*"You're such a mess. You smell like
alcohol." She noticed.*

*"I went to this Skittles' party, and it was
fun."*

*"You went to a Skittles' party. Are you
crazy?" she shouted in my ear.*

"I needed to have a little fun, so I went."

*"You were out doing drugs and drinking
alcohol, while I was watching our baby. From the
looks of things, you smell like sex too." She began
to sob.*

*"Don't cry. I don't think I had sex with
anybody." I stood, trying to think, but I could only
laugh.*

*"You're high, Reagus. Let me get you to the
bathroom."*

*Joyce helped me to the bathroom and into
the shower. I stood there, shaking, as warm water
hit my body. After a few minutes, I sat down in the
shower, as the water pounded my chest, and went to
sleep.*

*Laying there, I felt kind of funny. Opening
my eyes, my body was floating, leaving my body. I
could see myself looking back at myself and walking
away. I went into the room with Joyce, as I saw she
was changing Brady's diaper. He was fussing and*

crying. As I stood there, staring, she gave him a bottle of milk.

"What are you doing here?" I asked, as she jumped around to face me.

"I came over to check on you. And luckily, I did. You were all messed up," she spoke, as she walked up to me. She continued, "I need to go pull your truck in. You left it running down by the black gate."

"How did you get in here?"

"Remember, I told you the black gate was open, and your front door was open too. That Skittles' party had you all kinds of messed up." She smiled, as she kissed me on the cheek. "I need to go get your truck from the gate."

Joyce walked off, leaving me there, naked. I looked over at Brady, as he looked back at me. His eyes seemed black and evil. Turning my attention away from Brady, I followed Joyce outside. This time, I didn't have to struggle to walk, but it seemed like my body was floating wherever I stepped.

Walking outside, naked, I could see Joyce walking toward the black gate. My truck was down there, and the high beams were on. Walking toward the lights, Joyce pulled the truck up and then went out to lock the gate back. She resumed inside the truck, as I walked to it. She drove past me, as I watched.

"Why did you walk off and leave Brady? He's by himself," she screamed at me, as I walked back to her.

"You shouldn't be here."

"Well, I am here. As I said, I came to check on you since you haven't seen your child in three days," Joyce stated.

"Three whole days. Get the fuck out of here." I laughed again. This time, it was a full-blown laugh.

Suddenly, Joyce slapped me across the face with all her might. Something snapped in me at that moment. It reminded me of Nurse Bessie at the East Mississippi Mental Institution.

Without thinking, I punched her in the face. Joyce fell to the ground. I guess she was in shock because she just stared at me. I tried to grab her, but she began kicking me violently. Jumping on top of her, I kept punching her in the face until it sounded like her nose cracked. As she screamed for dear life, I held her head and ripped her eyes out of their sockets. She tried to pry my hands away, but I dug them out.

Retrieving her eyes, I shoved them into my mouth and began to chew, as blood and fluid oozed down my chin. Bending over her, I began eating her face from her body. After a few minutes, my body floated back inside the house, dragging her body. I tied up Joyce and placed her into the oven. Turning

*the stove on to four hundred degrees, I left her there
to cook.*

*Floating back into the living room, I
snatched the bottle out of Brady's mouth. He
immediately started screaming. Grabbing him by
his little throat, I choked him to death. Dropping his
body to the ground like a heavy sack of potatoes, I
floated back to the bathroom. I could see my body
laying there, lifeless. Getting back inside to join the
rest of me, I fell asleep.*

*Early that morning, I woke up to the cold
shower still hitting me. It had turned cold, and I was
shaking badly. Lifting my stiff body from the tub, I
turned off the water and heard a baby crying.
Everything seemed like a dream. I remembered
being at the Skittles' party, and then, I appeared
home. Didn't know how I got home from Decatur to
Steeletown. Then, I remember Joyce coming over
with Brady. That baby kept screaming out.*

*"Joyce, Brady is crying. What are you
doing?" I yelled out, as I got a towel and dried off.
"Joyce," I screamed again. It smelled like she was
in the kitchen. "Joyce, what the hell are you doing?
Get that baby," I screamed once again, as I exited
the bathroom to spot a trail of blood.*

*Looking at the big trails of blood, I went to
the kitchen. Joyce wasn't in there, but the stove was
on. I opened the oven and jumped back. Joyce was*

laying in the stove, burnt. Her body was burnt to a crisp.

"What did I do?" I asked myself, as I began to cry and stare at Joyce. I sat there for a few minutes, then I remembered Brady.

When I jumped up to find him, his dead body lay in the living room, half eaten. "Brady, no," I screamed, as I rushed over and picked Brady up off the ground like a delicate flower.

Tears fell down my face like a water faucet, as I held his dead body. His leg was gone, his stomach was ripped open, and half his face was gone.

"Oh, God, what have I done? I thought it was a dream; I thought it was a dream," I shouted out to myself, as I held Brady close.

I cried and cried until no more tears fell down my face. I had been sitting there for hours, holding Brady, until Uncle Earl showed up. He walked through the house and jumped back when he saw me. I glanced at him then began staring back at the wall.

"Reagus, what in the hell happened?" Uncle Earl asked, as he walked around, staring at me.

"I don't know," I managed to say.

"You realize you are holding your baby. He's dead," he slowly spoke.

"I don't know what happened. I went to this party last night, and then, I woke up here at the house. Joyce helped me in the shower, then my body was floating around everywhere," I started, knowing he probably wouldn't believe me.

"Your body was floating." He smirked.

"Yes, my body was floating all over the house. I was in the tub, and I could see myself walking through the house," I explained.

"You must have taken some strong drugs or something?"

"Yes, I was at the party, and we all popped pills and drank alcohol. The kids there mixed a bunch of pills, and we took them."

"Damn, Reagus." He shook his head.

"I don't even remember how I got home last night. I went from the party to here." I quivered, as tears fell down my face.

"Let me help you clean up this mess," Uncle Earl offered, as he tried to grab Brady from my arms.

"No, just leave him," I shouted.

"Okay, what's that smell?" he asked, as he stood and walked to the kitchen.

"That's Joyce," I whispered, but he didn't hear me.

"Oh, shit," he shouted out, and I closed my eyes.

I felt him walking back into the living room, then he spoke. "I am going to help you clean up in here."

"Yes, sir," I stated, as I looked down at Brady and cradled him.

I rocked him all day until Uncle Earl came back. He slowly picked up Brady from my arms and carried him out the back door. Standing on my feet, I walked to the back door. Uncle Earl put Brady and what was left of Joyce's body into the Brazen Bull barbecue grill. He put lighter fluid on them and burned them.

After a long, hot shower, I cleaned up. Dipping the ashes out of the grill, I buried them in a grave with pink and yellow rose bushes. Sitting there, staring at those roses, was the most devastating moment of my life.

After that day, I had Uncle Earl call the police on me. I decided to give myself up. I couldn't believe I killed my son.

CHAPTER 8

(Labor Day Slaughter)

Dr. Amanda Smith asked, "When and why did you decide to share your secret with Kale and Kyle?"

"Because they were hungry. The more I fed them, the hungrier they got. I had to tell them where it came from. Kale didn't accept it at first, but she got onboard with me, and Kyle was too excited. After I told them, they became a menace to society. They were after their favorite meat but more violent than me," I responded.

Occurred Incident: FAMILY SECRET

Picking up Amber Rose, I stared at her ugly face for a few minutes until she drooled on my hand. My mind wanted to toss her across the room for drooling on me, but the hairs on the back of my neck began to stand tall. My tongue hung from my mouth, and slob lingered, dripping onto my shirt. Wiping my mouth and cradling her in my arms like a baby should be, I began sniffing her. Her smell reminded me so much of Bonnie Logan. At that moment, I knew she had to be eaten. Today was her day to die.

As I walked back into the kitchen holding Amber Rose, she cried, as I fixed her a bottle of milk. I poured a half bottle of Benadryl into the bottle as well. Feeding Amber Rose made my stomach growl. At first, I felt light-headed at the thought of eating my baby sister. But that feeling quickly faded.

After I fed her, I gave her a warm bath, hoping it would help put her to sleep fast. Amber Rose indeed fell asleep before I finished her bath. I sniffed her every chance I got. Her sweet smell had mesmerized me. I couldn't take it anymore; I had to taste her. Releasing her sleeping body in the water, I proceeded to my mother's room and got John's hunting knife. Staring at the knife, I undressed myself down to my underwear because I knew there would be a mess. I should have just eaten her right there. Entering the bathroom, I began tearing off her meat, piece by piece, because I knew the others were going to be hungry later.

I didn't know if she was dead or not from all the Benadryl I gave her, but I knew she never woke up. Before I carved her to pieces, I dried her off and began eating right there. Ripping off piece after piece, I was in Heaven. This was the first time I could enjoy eating what I had been craving for years. After pleasing myself with delicious bites, I began to carve her feet off and tossed them into the garbage bag. Then, cutting off her small hands and decapitating her head from her body, I tossed them into the garbage bag. Carving her body to pieces in the bathtub, so I would not get blood everywhere, I continued to eat more of her, then I placed the rest in the garbage bag. Finally, I sliced her into many pieces, so I could roast her.

After the carving of Amber Rose, I put her mutilated body in a big roasting pan. Running to my bedroom, I took out a bag of Irish potatoes I had hidden in the closet from Mother. Slicing ten potatoes with a whole onion and bell peppers, I seasoned the pieces with Lawry seasoned sauce and Worcestershire sauce. It was time for my dish.

Putting Pam cooking spray around the pan to make sure it didn't stick, like you would regular meat, I placed the mutilated baby inside. Placing the lid over the food, I turned the stove on to four hundred degrees. As Amber Rose cooked, I placed the other parts into almost eight garbage bags. After putting on more clothes, I left the apartment with a big bag of garbage and a bleach bottle. Walking to the back of the apartment complex to the dumpster, I saw two little kids playing, so I had to run them off. They cursed me like they were grown, and I promised to beat their tails if I saw them again. At the dumpster, I opened the garbage bag and poured the whole bottle of bleach into it. The bleach leaked out, but I poured it until it was empty. Tying the bag up, I threw the bag of garbage away with the empty bleach bottle. Looking around to see if anyone was looking, I dusted my pants off and rushed back to the apartment.

After I finished baking Amber Rose, I just had to taste a piece before Kyle and Kale got there. OMG… she tasted so good. Better than Bonnie Logan. Before I could eat another piece, Kyle and Kale rushed through the door with their eyes open wide.

"Something smells so good," Kale called out, as she made her way to the kitchen.

"I'm ready to eat. What are we having?" Kyle asked, as he tossed his bookbag on the floor, heading into the kitchen.

"We are having roast and cake. I need some rice and gravy. Can y'all wait?"

"I don't want no rice. I'm hungry now," Kyle yelled out while sitting at the kitchen table.

"Why don't you two start on your homework, and I will prepare some rice? I bought some rice in a bag, so it will take about ten minutes. And it won't take long for the gravy," I stated, as I began to prepare the rice and gravy.

"Homework? I don't have any," Kyle smarted off.

"Yeah, right. Do your work, and I will let you eat until you can't eat no more," I stated.

Kyle's eyes lit up like a Christmas tree. He was ready to chop down. As they did homework in the living room, I finished preparing the rice and gravy. Kyle kept looking into the kitchen like he was starving to death. Truth was, he might be starving. If he only knew.

After I finished everything, we all sat down for the first time as a family and began to eat. I put the rice on the table while placing chunks of meat and gravy over it. We all sat there and ate Amber Rose. I moaned every time I took a bite. The meat was so delicious.

"Where's Amber Rose?" Kale asked.

"Robin took her when she came by here stealing our food out of the refrigerator," I responded without looking at her. I wanted to enjoy every single bite.

"Not again," Kyle replied, as he jumped up and opened the refrigerator. He continued, "We work so hard to get it."

"I know, Kyle. We had a long talk. I don't think she will do it again."

"I hope not because I'm getting tired of this," he replied while sitting back down to finish eating.

"Why does it smell like bleach in here?" Kale asked, as she chewed her meat.

"I cleaned up before I cooked. There was an awful smell in here."

"Oh, okay," she said, as she continued to eat up her food in a rush.

That day we ate and ate until our bellies couldn't take anymore. I had cleaned the entire apartment with bleach that night, as they slept. I cleaned up like I was a maid. I was so happy and very excited about my birthday. We ate Amber Rose for about three days until it was all gone. I ate the best meat ever, and I wasn't going to stop there. This was only the beginning of them tasting their favorite meat: human flesh.

SECOND INCIDENT

"Why is it that when you cook, it smells like bleach? Are you trying to kill us?" Kyle stated.

"No, I'm not trying to kill you. If I was, I would do it with my hands, not bleach," I replied. I continued, "I use the bleach to cover up the smell in here. I serve our favorite meat and can't be caught."

"What do you mean our favorite?" Kale asked.

"Promise you won't scream or go all crazy on me," I replied.

"You probably feeding us people," Kale stated, as she laughed.

"Yes, that's what it is, human meat."

"Stop playing. Are you feeding up human meat?" Kale asked.

"I'm serious."

"Reagus, are you feeding us people?" Kyle asked this time

"I told you yes. Don't freak out on me," I stated.

"I told you we were eating people. You didn't believe me," Kyle said to Kale.

"If it is people, that shit tastes good." Kale laughed.

"No cussing," I interrupted.

"Damn, I can't believe we are eating people," Kyle said.

"How are you getting this meat?" Kale asked.

"I must kill them. Some with my bare hands and others with medication," I explained.

"So, you're a serial killer now?" Kale laughed.

"If that's what you want to call it. I'm just eating my favorite meat. And, by the looks of it, you two are enjoying it yourselves. You want seconds and thirds."

"That's before I knew what it was," Kale replied.

"I don't care; I'm going to get some more meat. Have you cooked?" Kyle asked.

"Yes, I have."

"Let's eat. I'm hungry."

"Go wash your hands."

"I'm not eating no humans," Kale said.

"That's you. I'm hungry," Kyle replied, as he dried off his hands.

*I cooked roast beef with onions, potatoes,
English peas, and carrots laying on top of a bed of
rice. Kyle sat down and began eating immediately;
Kale just sat there, looking. I fixed her plate and put
it in front of her. She began eating everything
except the meat. Kyle finished his and wanted more.*

*"You better eat. You know Robin isn't going
to cook. We can't keep expecting Reagus to feed
us," Kyle told her.*

"I know."

*"You were eating it before, so eat it now. I
have an idea."*

"What idea?" I asked.

*I could see the look in Kyle's eyes. He
wanted more of his favorite meat. He'd never killed
before, but I bet he would just to eat.*

"Don't do anything stupid," I said to Kyle.

*"I'm going to do what you're doing, kill,"
Kyle remarked.*

"No, you're not," I replied.

"Who's going to stop me?"

*Before we could continue, Kale was eating
her food like she hadn't eaten in days. I smiled at
her then frowned at Kyle.*

"Don't do it. You've never killed before."

*"So, I'm going to start. I want to eat more,"
Kyle remarked.*

"Let me provide it and you just eat."

*"Hell no. I'm killing me a mother…" Kyle
stated.*

"Kyle!" I interrupted.

*Kyle jumped up and walked out. Kale was
licking the plate. I gave her another huge plate, and
she ate. Afterward, she went to join Kyle on the
front porch. I shouldn't have said anything because
Kyle was going to be a problem.*

THIRD INCIDENT

*Sitting at home, watching television, I heard
something. Turning off the television, I walked
closer to my front window. The barn light was on
the outside. I put on my shoes and ran out. I
couldn't let the others know what I was doing.
Instead of slaughtering hogs, I was doing humans.*

*Opening the barn door, Kale was standing
back, as Kyle was bashing in someone's head with a
hammer.*

*"What the fuck is going on here? Kyle!" I
yelled.*

*"What?" Kyle yelled out, as he stopped with
the hammer in midair.*

*"You can't do that here. This is a kid.
Someone will be looking for him," I said.*

*"Nobody looking for this reject. He's
homeless and stupid," Kyle remarked.*

"Are you sure?" Kale spoke with a soft cry.

"You know this reject. He's a waste. But too late, he's dead." Kyle laughed.

"This shit ain't funny," I said.

"Reagus!" Kyle yelled.

"What?"

"He's dead now. Help me."

"Shit, Kyle," I harshly spoke.

Kyle lifted the hammer and continued to bash the teenager's head in. He fell to the ground like a sack of potatoes. You could tell he was still breathing because his back was rising and falling. Kyle had stripped him of his shirt. Kyle had become a savage right in front of my eyes. What was I going to do with him? When he got older, I wouldn't be able to stop him.

"Reagus, are you going to help me?" Kyle asked, as I snapped back to reality.

I helped him carve up the teenager. Kale stood back, as we worked, cutting this boy into pieces. Kyle took a bite out of him and began chewing.

"This tastes good without cooking it." Kyle chewed, as he handed Kale a piece. She ate it without hesitation. A few minutes later, Kale was down, eating the leg like she hadn't eaten in years again.

"Dang, girl, you are hungry," Kyle spoke.

"Leave her alone. You just enjoy yours. I'm taking a cut of this meat," I spoke.

"That's a big no," Kyle stated.

"But I helped you," I replied.

"It's still all mine and Kale's. We got him up here."

"Yeah, without letting me know you were coming up here. You used my place; I get some of that meat," I stated.

"Okay, I will give you an arm, but that's it, nothing else," Kyle harshly spoke.

"I will take that."

We devoured half of the meat. We pulled the meat from the bones, and I planted them under a red rock crape tree. Kale and Kyle helped me plant the tree since they caused all this drama. Afterward, we wrapped the meat in aluminon foil. Kale was still eating, as we wrapped the meat. She loved our favorite meat.

CHAPTER 9

(Thanksgiving Feast)

Dr. Amanda Smith asked, "What thoughts crossed your mind as you killed some of your family members at a Thanksgiving feast?"

"I premeditated my family's murders. I invited both sides of the family for a huge Thanksgiving feast, even though I knew they weren't going to show up. For the ones that showed up, I saved their lives and gave them money. The others were sentenced to death."

Occurred Incident: HAPPY THANKSGIVING

Standing next to my belladonna plants, I put on my garden gloves and began picking the blackberries from their leaves. Dropping the blackberries inside a plastic bag, I began to think about this new wine I'd decided to prepare. It would be sweet from the blackberries and bitter from the wine.

After hours of picking and washing the blackberries, I added them to the wine and blood I had already mixed up. Grinding all the contents together, I strained them into the empty Chardonnay bottles I collected. Each bottle was carefully prepared with a cork to seal the deal. It took me all day to prepare the wine.

Afterward, I went to Kroger to buy all my cakes and pies, but I prepared the main ingredients myself. Tomorrow morning would be my first Thanksgiving dinner as a family. Hopefully, everyone would show up.

"Is all the food ready?" Uncle Earl asked, as he stood in my kitchen, ready to eat.

"Yes, Uncle Earl, everything is cooked. I'm just waiting for everybody to show up."

"I hate to disappoint you, but maybe one or two will show up. You know your Aunt Ellen and her greedy kids are coming. Your Aunt Renee might come with her family. The rest of them aren't coming here," Uncle Earl explained.

"Just them few are better than none. Help me set the table before anybody gets here," I stated, as I began preparing the table.

"Seems like we spoke her up. There is your Aunt Ellen and her crew. Kids already looking like they're starving to death." Uncle Earl laughed.

"Stop it." I laughed too, as I walked to the front door to greet them.

"Hello, everybody," I greeted, as Aunt Ellen, her new boyfriend, Ben, and her three children approached the door.

"Hey, Reagus, it's been a long time since I saw you," Aunt Ellen greeted me, as she hugged me tight and planted a kiss on my cheek. Her hug felt genuine.

"Hey, Reagus," Ben mumbled. He looked like Aunt Ellen dragged him over here. The kids smiled at me. The boy, Trey, gave me a dirty look.

"Uncle Earl and I were just about to set the table. Everybody, head to the kitchen," I announced, as I saw another car enter the driveway.

Slowly driving up, I saw Aunt Renee and her husband, Dale. They parked and exited the car with their son, DJ.

"Hey, Aunt Renee. Uncle Dale, come on in," I greeted with a big smile. I was the happiest person on Earth at that moment.

I had never had an actual Thanksgiving dinner in my life before. I'd looked at lots of YouTube videos. This was a very special day for me. Nobody knew exactly how special this day was to me.

"You look more and more like your daddy." Aunt Renee smiled, as she gave me a big hug, not wanting to let go. Uncle Dale had to clear his throat for her to let me go. Their son, DJ, gave me a big hug then Uncle Dale. I was very happy.

"Well, come in. I have cooked up a little of everything. Head on to the kitchen." I laughed, as I walked behind them. Uncle Earl was standing at the entrance of the kitchen, waving to them to come in.

"Hey, Renee. Dale." Uncle Earl greeted them, as he hugged them both. DJ went around them, avoiding the hug.

"Hey, Ellen. I should have known your hungry butt was going to be here," Aunt Renee smarted off, as she looked at Aunt Ellen and rolled her eyes.

"Yeah." Aunt Ellen greeted her back.

It seemed like the two ladies had bad blood between them. Everybody else greeted each other and sat down.

"I hope others show up," I mentioned, as I looked out the dining room window.

"Ain't nobody coming over here," Aunt Ellen smarted off. Ben bumped her arm, and they stared at each other for a few seconds.

"Why not?" I asked.

Everyone started staring at each other. It made me feel uneasy. Uncle Earl gave me that look.

"What's wrong with coming over here?" I asked again, as I looked at Aunt Renee and Aunt Ellen.

"Well, everybody has been talking nonsense about you, and they feel uncomfortable coming over here," Aunt Renee tried to explain.

"What she is trying to say is they are all talking about you, saying you eating people," DJ spoke without thinking.

"DJ!" Uncle Dale called out.

"Well, it's the truth. They are all talking about him," DJ stated, as he looked at me.

"Really, DJ? Sounds like they don't know what they're talking about. I don't understand why people take stuff the wrong way. I was ten years old when I bit that girl's leg, and I was punished. You mean to tell me that my own family is punishing me too," I spoke out, as everyone looked at me.

"We are here, baby. Don't worry about what the rest of them are talking about," Aunt Renee stated.

"Renee, you were talking about the boy too," Aunt Ellen blurted out.

"You're a liar, Ellen. That was you and that nasty mouth Ben talking about Reagus like he was an animal," Aunt Renee replied, as she pointed her finger at them across the table.

"So, we were curious just like y'all," Aunt Ellen spoke.

"That's a lie, Ellen. We love Regus. You two are here because of the money," Aunt Renee stated.

"Liar," Aunt Ellen screamed.

The two women stood up as if they were ready to fight. Uncle Earl jumped up.

"Sit y'all asses down and enjoy this Thanksgiving dinner. Reagus didn't have to cook y'all nothing, but he did. This will be his first Thanksgiving with family, and y'all messing it up," Uncle Earl stated.

Everybody turned to look at me.

"We're sorry, Reagus," Aunt Renee apologized, as she rushed over and hugged me. I hugged her back.

"It's okay, Aunt Renee. I didn't know people were talking about me like that."

"Not just people but your supposed to be family members," DJ blurted out again.

"DJ, if you say one more thing, I'm going to beat you," Aunt Renee threatened.

"Which is the human meat?" DJ blurted out again.

"DJ!" Aunt Renee shouted, as she popped him upside the head.

"I was just kidding." He laughed.

"Try the turkey. It's more like human meat." I laughed.

"Reagus!" Aunt Renee shouted.

"I'm just kidding, Aunt Renee." I laughed.

"We're out of here," Aunt Ellen shouted, as she gathered Ben and the kids.

"Aunt Ellen, don't leave. There isn't any human meat on my table. I was just kidding with DJ." I frowned, hoping she wouldn't leave.

"Joke or not, you were serious. We're not about to eat no damn people," she shouted, as they headed out the door. Aunt Ellen's oldest child, Trey, just sat there.

"Let's go, Trey," Aunt Ellen shouted.

"I'm hungry. I'm not leaving until I eat. I don't care if it's people or not. I'm not leaving until I eat."

"Get your butt up and let's go," Aunt Ellen threatened.

"Goodbye, Ellen, I'm not going until I eat." Trey harshly spoke to his mom.

"Fine, you will walk home," Aunt Ellen stated.

"It won't be the first time," he smarted off.

Aunt Ellen kept walking out the front door. I wanted to stop her, but Uncle Earl gave me that look again. I couldn't tell what he was saying, but whatever it was probably wasn't good.

"Can we please eat?" Trey asked.

"Yes, we can go ahead and eat," I replied.

"Thank you. I have never had Thanksgiving dinner either, Reagus. I'm happy you invited us over. Mama and the rest of them gossiping hens were talking about whether to come over here or not. They had a long meeting this morning about it. I didn't care if I had to walk over here; I was coming," Trey explained, as he smiled at me.

Aunt Renee said a small prayer, and we all ate Thanksgiving dinner. Even though it was a small crowd, I was happy. We all talked and laughed. It felt good. Suddenly, a car pulled up. Headed to the front door, Aunt Ellen was back. She walked right on in and hugged me.

"I'm so sorry for being stupid toward you, Reagus. Please forgive me," Aunt Ellen apologized.

"I forgave you the moment you walked out my door," I lied.

"Can we please join you all for dinner?" she asked.

"Come on back in and eat."

Aunt Ellen and her other two kids, minus Ben, sat at the table and ate. We all continued to talk and have fun. Aunt Renee had brought a few board games. That was one of the best times of my life.

After Thanksgiving Day, I gathered my Chardonnay wine, and Uncle Earl and I headed out to deliver it to my other relatives that didn't show up for my Thanksgiving dinner.

"I don't understand why you insist on giving these fools something. They didn't show up yesterday; therefore, they deserve nothing." Uncle Earl frowned, as he drove the van.

"Just let it go, Uncle Earl. I have a master plan," I stated, as I grinned at him.

"I hope your master plan work."

"It will work out. I'm just in the mood for giving. Can you just deal with that?"

"You, giving. I'm not seeing the point in this. When did you become Mr. Santa Claus, giving gifts and shit?" Uncle Earl sarcastically spoke.

"It is just wine, Uncle Earl." I laughed.

"You could give them wines to me instead. These mutherfuckers don't care about you or your wine," he replied with a little bass in his voice.

"It's okay. Just let it go," I replied. I didn't want to tell him my plan. I continued, "I will give you a couple of bottles and money when we finish. You know I always do you right."

"Yes, you do, and I know my brothers and sisters don't deserve wine. You have been too generous this holiday season."

"I am giving them wine because they didn't get a chance to show up," I spoke, knowing that was a lie.

"I told you before you even cooked all that food."

"I'm just happy that somebody showed up. I enjoyed myself yesterday, didn't you?"

"Yes, I did have a little fun." He laughed.

"Me too. Too bad that was my first and last Thanksgiving dinner." I frowned, as I looked out the window, and Uncle Earl didn't say a word. He looked at me and kept driving.

Hours passed by, and we delivered all forty bottles except for one. Uncle Earl kept insisting on drinking it, but I told him no, that I had some at home. If only he knew that the wine was poisoned. The blackberries from the belladonna tree were poisonous if consumed with ten berries or more.

Finally, after delivering all the wine, nothing happened. I wanted bodies to fall off the earth, dead. But instead, I got nothing. They had to get rid of it, at least pouring it out or throwing away the whole bottle. My plan backfired on me. All I wanted was for my family to come to Thanksgiving dinner.

CHAPTER 10

(Christmas Mutilation)

Dr. Amanda Smith asked, "How could you kill hundreds of people, including your family?"

"You haven't heard a word I have said to you. I have no remorse for these people or their families. I kill to eat. Those people were nothing. If the police go to my property, they will see. All the beautiful, colored trees and plants represent a body. All the bones and leftover meat I didn't eat are buried underneath," I replied.

OCCURRED INCIDENT

Preparing my belladonna plants and berries for the soda drinks, I was contemplating putting the mashed-up berries and plants in the mashed potatoes. The belladonna plant was known as the "deadly nightshade". The berry of the plant was dangerous. Consumption of ten berries or more was fatal. But both leaves and roots had a sharp, unpleasant odor and bitter taste. I tried to find different foods to put the belladonna leaves and roots in.

Driving down the highway from Jackson to Meridian, I was careful not to waste the sodas.

Arriving, I met Tammie Steele, the owner of Steele Stewpot.

"Hello, Reagus, you're early," Tammie stated, as she hugged me. Her perfume stank, and it almost made me gag.

"Hi, Tammie."

"You're early."

"Yes, I am. I wanted to help you all prepare the food. I know you're short-staffed." I came back with an answer.

"That's so sweet of you. I could use the help. We will serve a little over a hundred people. I did a head count of all the homeless people that came in. There were about ninety-nine, but I added in a few plates for the others," she replied.

"That's wonderful. That's why we're here - to feed the needy," I said.

"They're going to love everything. I hear you brought some of your special sauce to go on the baked turkey."

"Yes, I did. It tastes a little bitter but adds a little sugar, and we shall be set," I mentioned, as I unloaded the truck.

Tammie and one of her helpers, John Webb, helped unload, so we could prepare to cook.

"I thought you were coming tomorrow," John said.

"I have to be in Tupelo, Mississippi at Weems Stewpot to help serve them and then to Gulfport, Mississippi to Cleveland Stewpot," I stated.

"You're going to be a very busy man these next few days. What about your family? You're not spending the holidays with them?"

"My mother and father aren't around. My twin sister and brother have disappeared from me, so I don't too much care about that. I will cook for my other family though. Hopefully, they will show up."

"Why wouldn't they show up?"

"I don't know. Crazy." I laughed.

"I feel you. I have a family the same way. Just crazy for no reason."

"What you two chatter boxes talking about?" Tammie spoke.

"Family, cooking for the holidays," John mentioned.

"Come on. We need to cook," Tammie said, as we unloaded the last bit.

Cooking the mashed potatoes, I decided not to add my ingredients to it. I already made some with the sauce and then put some in the drinks. I hadn't tested any of this on anybody. I had no idea how long it would take to put them down. I researched before I did anything, and it took me three to four hours.

After I finished cooking, we all served the food. Two other helpers were helping us. One girl kept wasting gravy on her hand and then licked it off. I was sweating, hoping this girl didn't pass out.

After serving about ninety-eight people, we shut down the center. The staff took plates home. They kept coming back for more to drink. All sodas went very quickly. There were about six homeless people laid out on the ground. Everyone just assumed they were full and laid out.

"Thank you, Reagus, for helping us," Tammie said.

"You're welcome. Why don't you look so good?"

"I don't know. I ate, and now my stomach is boiling."

"TMI, Tammie." I laughed.

"I'm just saying."

"Okay, well, I must go. I must arrive in Tupelo by tomorrow morning."

"Have a safe trip."

"I will. Thanks."

Tammie and I parted ways. I left and headed to Tupelo, Mississippi.

It took me three hours to finally get to Tupelo. I went by the Cleveland Stewpot to meet Regina Cleveland. There was stuff to be delivered.

"Hey," Regina said.

"Hello. Glad you were able to meet me this time of night."

"You better be glad you are helping; I won't be out this time of night for nobody. Especially this part of town," she madly stated.

"I apologize. I can prepare stuff, and you just leave. I'm sure I will find everything I need."

"Here are the keys and don't be late tomorrow. I have stuff to do."

"I won't be late," I replied.

Regina jumped in her Jeep and pulled off. I was looking at her keys to the stewpot in my hand and her Jeep speeding off.

"Well, thank you for a nice greeting," I said to myself, as I frowned.

Unloading the truck, I had a few homeless people come by and see what was going on. They didn't help but were nosey.

After unloading the truck, I began to cook the turkey and gravy. The mashed potatoes weren't hard. Regina had mac and cheese too. I'd let her cook that with her mean ass. The drinks were ready to serve with my belladonna juice from the roots and leaves.

Finishing up and storing food, I headed to my hotel. This was going to be a long day.

"Good morning," I spoke to Regina.

"Ya, morning to you," she replied with a stuck-up attitude.

"I cooked everything except the mac and cheese. I didn't know if you wanted me to cook it or not."

"Why would you think that? You cooked everything else."

"Well, maybe I was leaving it for you since you're so rude."

"Rude?"

"Yes, rude. You were rude last night, and you're rude now. I didn't have to come here to help. I volunteered."

"I apologize. I have so much on my plate, then I have dinner at home to prepare," she pointed out.

"I understand. That's why I am here. To help."

"Thank you and I apologize for being rude."

"You're welcome. Now, let's get this thing rolling," I spoke.

After preparing to serve, there were no helpers. Didn't anybody come to help? I was thinking maybe it was Regina's nasty attitude.

"I guess it's me and you," I stated, as I began to serve.

"Yes, it's hard to find good help without someone stealing."

"Stealing the food?"

"Yes, I guess to take home."

"That's sad."

"Yes, it is," Regina stated, as she stashed her plate back.

We served almost fifty-two people. Some came back for seconds, and we let them have it because nobody else showed up. I was kind of scared because I figured the belladonna juice would kick in faster than expected.

"You did a great job with the food. This gravy is a little bitter but good, especially with this mac and cheese."

"Glad you're enjoying it."

"Why aren't you eating?"

"I'm not hungry. I will grab something later."

"Are you sure? It's a little food left."

"I'm sure, but I must be going. I must head to Gulfport to help them. Who's going to help you clean up?"

"I will take my time and clean. There are a few homeless people that will help me clean up just for the rest of the food. Don't worry about us. You just get to Gulfport."

"Oh, yes. Tomorrow is Christmas Eve; I must be finished before my own family comes over."

"You're a very nice guy."

"Thank you."

"You go on and get out of here."

"Okay, nice meeting you."

"Nice meeting you as well."

I gathered a few things I brought and headed out. In a way, I was sleepy but had to get things together before my own family showed up. Everyone confirmed they would be there. I guess *they saw I didn't kill anyone at Thanksgiving. Thank God I didn't. My plan worked.*

Driving back to Jackson, I listened to music. That was something I rarely did. I hated music because of Robin. She would come home high and just blast the music. I hated rap music. This was some soft love music. It would set the mood for people who were in love. It took my mind back to Joyce. She was a very pretty, unique kind of girl. The love of my life. She would taste so good on a platter, but I needed her around to raise my son, Brady.

Arriving in Jackson, I stopped by Hutson's Fish House and Catering.

"Hello, Mr. Dune. I'm so happy to finally meet you in person," greeted a small, framed female named Doris. The smell of her made me sick to my stomach.

"I'm not feeling so well."

"Is everything okay?"

"Yes, I just need a little air," I lied, as I stepped back out the door. Luckily, the wind was blowing downward.

Gathering myself, a large-framed man named Eric approached me.

"Hello, Mr. Dune. You feel better?" Eric asked, as he placed his hand on my shoulder.

"Yes, sir, I am. I think it was that perfume that lady had on," I lied.

"Sorry about that. Do come in," Eric invited me.

"Thank you."

"We have everything ready to go for Christmas Day."

"Are you going to have enough help to set up? I don't want my family serving," I spoke.

"Oh, yes, sir, don't you worry about that. I have enough people to help," he responded, as he handed me the dinner list. "Here's everything that will be served."

Reading over the list, everything was in order. They had all those delicious pies and desserts. The main course looked good too, but I was thinking only of the desserts.

"Everything looks great. I'm happy to give you the job. Now, hopefully, it will taste as great," I stated.

"Everything will taste delicious. We deliver the best."

"I'm very happy to hear."

We finished up our conversation, and I took off. I had three hours and fifteen minutes before I got to my destination. My day had been very long.

It took me three hours and fifteen minutes to drive from Jackson to Weems Stewpot in Gulfport. It was a fast trip, especially listening to soft music.

"Welcome to Weems Stewpot, Reagus," Lola Faye Weems greeted with a big smile.

"Hello, thank you." I smiled back.

"We're glad to have you here at our facility."

"I'm glad to be here."

"Come in," she invited.

Stepping into the stewpot, it was very clean and neat. It smelled so good, like oranges and apples. The staff looked clean.

"Are you ready to help us serve? Or you could just drop the gravy and drinks off," Lola Faye asked.

"I'm here to help serve. The gravy is ready, and the bottled drinks are cold," I advised.

"We sure do appreciate you for helping. We've cooked the turkey, the mac and cheese, the chicken and dumplings with rolls."

"That sounds delicious. I would love to try the chicken and dumplings if some are left over," I replied.

"We have a little set aside for the staff. You sure can get some."

"Thank you."

We set up the line and began serving supper on Christmas Eve. I was excited because all these people would die by my hands. I didn't care if they had families or not. I just wanted to see my work carried out. The homeless people were eating like no tomorrow. I guess they were hungry and waiting for me to arrive.

They could have served them lunch before I got there. All I had was gravy and drinks. Turned out they didn't have anything to drink but water. There weren't that many bottles of water. They didn't want to serve the food without gravy to go on the turkey and mashed potatoes. Lola Faye was very neat and in order with everything. She wanted her holiday meal to be on point.

"Here are the chicken and dumplings you wanted to taste," Lola Faye stated, as she handed me a small plastic bowl.

I sat down and ate the entire bowl.

"Do you have a jug of milk?" I asked Lola Faye.

The staff was sitting down with me, eating. Everyone was talking about Christmas and the snow that had started to fall.

"Here is the jug of milk. What are you going to do with it?" Lola Faye asked, as she handed me the jug.

"I'm a little thirsty and going to drink it." I laughed.

I took the lid off and began drinking like I hadn't drank anything in years. The staff looked at me like I had lost my mind.

"That was delicious," I stated, as I put down the half jug of milk.

My thought was the chicken and dumplings had my favorite gravy in them, but they did not. As the staff went back to eating, one of the homeless people fell out onto the ground, then another, then another.

"What in the world is going on? Call an ambulance," Lola Faye demanded.

One of the staff members took out her cell phone and dialed 911. I was in a panic now and ready to go. The belladonna plant worked faster on this set of homeless people. I was thinking it was because the gravy had time to sit and marinate.

The ambulance arrived, and all three were announced DOA (dead on arrival). A staff member fell out but was sent to the hospital.

"There has got to be something wrong with the food," I said.

"Why would you say that?" Lola Faye asked.

"All of them are dead after eating."

"I don't think anything is wrong with the food. Probably something else. We've had something like this happen before. They found nothing. They tested our food and nothing. I don't understand what could be wrong," Lola Faye explained.

"This has happened before, dang," I said with joy but didn't let her know I was happy. Now, it was my time to exit.

"Well, I would stay, Mrs. Weems, but I have to get back home and prepare my meal."

"I understand. Thank you for coming down to help us. Your help was very much appreciated."

"You're welcome. I love helping," I lied.

"You have a safe trip back."

"I will. Thank you," I said, as I exited.

My heart was racing like never before. I just knew I was exposed. I didn't want them to capture me. I had so much to do.

Driving back to Jackson, I drove in silence. My mind was on how many homeless people I had killed. I was wondering how many of them had died yet. I wanted to call and check, but I didn't want to be obvious.

Christmas morning had arrived, and I was up early, waiting for the catering company to show up. I told everyone that dinner would start at noon. I cooked my famous banana pudding with thallium poisoning. Everyone loved banana pudding except Aunt Wanda. The thallium poisoning was colorless and odorless, and nobody would taste it. I couldn't poison nothing else because the catering staff would be all over it.

After they set up, Uncle Earl and I went outside to wait for the guests to arrive.

"Do you think anybody will show up?" he asked.

"Most definitely. I had them all confirm they were coming. I'm shocked, but that's probably

because nothing happened to anyone at Thanksgiving."

"You're right about that. You planned this out carefully, but why?" he asked.

"I want them all dead. They knew that Raymond and Robin were treating me wrong and chose to do nothing about it. What if Raymond would have molested me as he wanted?" I spoke.

"Well, it didn't happen. Robin might have been a whore, but she wouldn't have let Raymond hurt you."

"No, she didn't. She just let him abandon us."

"Maybe that's why he left."

"Maybe but I don't care now. They both are dead," I replied.

"What about the children? Your cousins."

"What about them?"

"You do realize you plan to take the whole family out."

"Yes, I do realize. I thought about the kids, but I have no remorse. I don't care about those kids. I don't know them, and they don't know me. I have no feelings for them," I explained, as the first car pulled up.

"It's showtime," Uncle Earl spoke.

"Game time."

As we smiled and walked down to greet the first car, it was Uncle William with his wife, Pam, and daughter, Sunny.

"Hello, Reagus," Uncle William greeted, as he exited the car.

Aunt Pam looked all crazy, like someone was about to kill her off. It was true but not right now. Then, Sunny exited. She was a friendly child.

"Hey, Reagus," Sunny greeted.

"Hello, Sunny. Aunt Pam," I spoke.

"Hey, Reagus," Aunt Pam slowly greeted.

"Sunny, nice to finally meet you," I spoke, as she greeted me with a hug.

"You have done a lot to Mom and Dad's place. Looks so inviting and lovely," Uncle William spoke, as he patted me on the back. He continued, "Hey, Earl."

"Ya, William," Uncle Earl said.

"Come into my home," I invited, as everyone entered.

Another car was pulling up. "Uncle Earl, take them to the kitchen and seat them," I requested, as I greeted the next car.

Uncle Thomas pulled up in his new Lexus. "Reagus," he yelled out, as he exited his car.

"Uncle Thomas, glad to see you again."

"It has been a long time but happy to see you."

"Please do come in."

"Thank you."

We turned and looked at another car approaching.

"That looks like Renee's car," Uncle Thomas stated.

"It's her. She was here Thanksgiving."

"Sorry I couldn't make it to Thanksgiving dinner."

"It's okay. You are here now. Family time," I warmly stated.

Uncle Thomas walked into the house, as Uncle Earl greeted him and directed him to the kitchen. I opened Aunt Renee's car door, as she unfastened her seatbelt.

"Reagus, my sweet baby," Aunt Renee stated, as her speech slurred.

She was so drunk she could barely stand up. I took her hand and guided her toward the house.

"Thank you, Reagus," Uncle Dale thanked. He was Aunt Renee's husband.

"It's no problem, Uncle Dale."

"Come on in, DJ," Uncle Dale told their teenage son.

"I'm coming. Don't rush me," he spat back.

"Bring your ass on in here before I take off my belt," Uncle Dale threatened.

"Ya, ya," DJ replied, as he marched into the house.

Uncle Earl guided them in, as I seated Aunt Renee.

"Reagus, the baby, give me a glass of wine," Aunt Renee requested.

"You've had enough, Renee. Let it go. Nobody has time for your bullshit today. We're here to enjoy family," Uncle Dale stated.

"You can kiss my ass, Dale. You haven't done that in a long damn time."

"Whatever, sloppy drunk," Dale remarked.

"Don't forget children are in here," Uncle William let her know.

"Shut up, William," Aunt Renee shot back.

"Excuse me, someone else is pulling up," I said, excusing myself. Walking back outside in the cold air, Aunt Ellen showed up with Ben, her boyfriend, and her son, Trey. She didn't bring the other two children. By this time, Joyce showed up with my son, Brady. Everything looked great. My plan was going as I desired it except for one thing. How the hell was I going to get Joyce out of there in time for the dessert?

As Joyce and Brady entered, Aunt Wanda and her team came in. She had her husband, Terrell, with her son, Dan, and two daughters, Jamie and Tyler.

"Hey, Aunt Wanda," I greeted with a huge smile. I could tell she was Raymond's twin sister. They were of different sexes but looked just alike.

"Reagus, hey." She hugged me.

"Please come in. Everyone is here and ready to eat."

"I'm hungry myself."

"Hello, everyone, welcome to my home. Some of you grew up here, and some of you have visited here. I hate Grandma and Grandpa aren't with us, but they are in spirit," I spoke before I was interrupted.

"We don't want to hear the bullshit. I'm ready to eat," Aunt Renee said.

"Here we go,' Uncle Thomas spoke in his soft voice.

"Thomas, don't get me started on your sweet ass," Aunt Renee remarked.

"Go ahead, boo, get it started," Uncle Thomas said as he stood, snapping his fingers.

"Let's not fight. I want this to be a joyful moment."

"Can we eat? I'm hungry," Trey spoke.

"Yes, we can, but let us pray," I stated.

"Keep it short and sweet," Aunt Pam spoke slowly.

"Yes, Aunt Pam. First and foremost, I would like to thank God for the food we are about to receive, and to my family, thank you all for coming to join me. Amen," I prayed quickly.

"That was short." Sunny laughed.

"Your mom said short and sweet." I laughed.

Everyone began eating and talking. Uncle William and Uncle Thomas were trying to talk about their sister, Renee, and she wasn't having it. Uncle Dale just ate. It was like this was a constant problem with the family at gatherings. Aunt Pam didn't say much. The kids looked and ate.

"Shut the fuck up," Uncle Earl yelled out. He continued, "Reagus set up a nice family dinner for everybody, and y'all acting like idiots. Especially you, Renee. You've been drunk ever since you got here. Sit your ass down and shut up."

"Dale, you going to let him talk to me like that?" Aunt Renee stated to Uncle Dale.

"He's right. Every time we have a get together, you always be drunk."

"Fuck you too, Dale," Aunt Renee shouted.

"Can I have some banana pudding?" Sunny asked, as she moved her plate over.

"Sure, I was hoping we all could eat it together. It's Grandma's recipe," I remarked.

"Mama didn't have no recipes," Uncle Thomas remarked.

"Mama had plenty of cookbooks, especially her own she made up for us during the holidays," Aunt Wanda replied, as she twisted in her seat.

"Why didn't I get a book?" Uncle Thomas questioned.

"Probably because she didn't know you were a fairy." Aunt Renee laughed.

"You nasty-looking heffa." Uncle Thomas frowned.

"Don't call me no…" Aunt Renee replied before I cut her off.

"Excuse me, excuse me, but I would like to introduce you all to my son, Brady, and his mother, Joyce."

"What's the point?" Aunt Ellen remarked.

"The point is I want my family to know me and my family. I only met you all during my childhood. I had one or two of you visit me in that mental institution. Yes, I said it. I'm not ashamed," I stated, as I continued to stand tall.

"I was coming to see you in that place," Uncle Thomas said. He continued, "I just couldn't do it. No kid should be in a place like that."

"I agree. That was my reason," Aunt Wanda and Aunt Ellen stated.

"It's okay. I understand. I was just ten years old. A child that needed his family. A child that needed someone to stand up and fight for him, but that's over with now," I said, as I sat down.

"What we all are saying, Reagus, is that we're sorry. Does everyone agree?" Uncle William spoke, as he stood up and hugged me.

"It's okay, Uncle William."

"Y'all mutherfuckers don't care about Reagus. Nobody helped him, not even me. If I hadn't been down the road I was headed, I would have taken him," Uncle Earl stated.

"You mean down the road you are going now." Aunt Renee laughed.

"Ya, Earl, don't act like you the good one," Uncle Thomas remarked.

"Let's not name call. Everyone is okay. I'm out and grown now. Please enjoy your food, so we can have dessert," I replied.

"Yes, I want some banana pudding," Sunny stated.

"Me too," Jamie and Tyler said together.

After eating our Christmas dinner, Uncle Earl and I cleared the table. We placed three big punch bowls filled with banana pudding on the table. Everyone's eyes got big, especially the children. All of them seemed like good children, but I was once a good child. I was punished, so I wouldn't feel bad about them being punished.

"Reagus, I must be going. I must stop by my mother's house," Joyce spoke.

"Of course. I will walk you out," I replied, as I got up and walked Joyce out.

"It was nice meeting everyone," Joyce remarked.

"I'm sorry you saw my family act like that. I had no idea it was so many underlying issues."

"You should meet my family." She laughed.

"You can tell me the war stories later," I said, as I kissed her on the cheek then kissed Brady. He was sound asleep.

I watched Joyce and Brady ride down the road, as I walked back to join my so-called, fucked-up family.

"What happened?" I spoke, as I entered, and Uncle Dale was carrying Aunt Renee to the couch.

"She's drunk. I'll let her sleep it off before we head out," Uncle Dale stated, as he placed Aunt Renee on the couch and sat next to her.

"You're not having any banana pudding?" I asked.

"You're late. I've had two helpings." He laughed.

"That was quick." I laughed.

Before I could walk out, Uncle Dale was out next to Aunt Renee. Stepping into the kitchen, bodies were laid out everywhere except for Jamie, Aunt Wanda's daughter. She didn't eat banana pudding.

"What's wrong with everybody?" she cried.

"They're sleeping. Maybe you should go to sleep too."

"But I'm not sleepy."

Uncle Earl and I looked at each other. He hunched his shoulders, and I did mine. I had no

*idea what to do. At least she was not a teenager,
someone I would have to fight. She was a ten-year-
old girl that needed someone to help her.*

"What are we going to do with her?"

*"I don't know. Just get out back and start
the barnyard fire. We must get rid of these bodies."*

"You're not enjoying any of them?"

"Why? You want some?"

"Hell no, not me."

"Okay then, get that fire started."

*I began helping Uncle Earl carry the bodies
out the back door. The thing about that was no
blood and no guts. Just dead bodies everywhere.*

*After all the bodies were outside and under
the big planks and pine trees, Uncle Earl lit the fire
with a little help from gasoline. He jumped back
quickly before the fire got him. He was playing and
almost lost his life.*

"What were you doing?" I yelled.

"I was trying to start the fire."

"You damn near killed yourself."

"Shit."

"You almost." I laughed. We both laughed.

*"What about the girl? What are we going to
do with her?"*

"Throw her in the fire," I ordered.

*"Not me. That girl is still alive. You do it,"
he replied.*

"I told you to do it."

"And I told you I wasn't. You're the heartless one."

"Don't act like you aren't."

"I didn't say I was," he replied.

I went into the house and snapped Jamie's neck then carried her lifeless body to the fire and threw her in. The fire lit up higher and then went back to a steady pace. That was it. Raymond's brothers and sisters were dead, along with their children.

All I could do was give a smile that turned into laughter, as Uncle Earl walked off.

CHAPTER 11

(No Control)

Dr. Amanda Smith asked, "Why did you attempt to burn down the East Mississippi Mental Institution?"

"Somehow, I knew you were going to come back around to this question. You just couldn't resist. But since we have established a small relationship, I will tell you," I replied.

Occurred Incident: *BURNING DOWN MEMORIES*

At ten years old, I was afraid and scared out of my mind waking up at a place such as the East Mississippi Mental Health Behavior Center. My first night cries rang throughout the floor we were on. To be exact, it was on the second floor. I thought it would be dark and a piss-like mess, but it wasn't. It was like a normal bedroom – one bed, one dresser, and a deck mounted on the wall with a chair. I had a shower and toilet in the room, and there were no cameras.

"If you don't stop all that crying, I will cut your tongue out your mouth and throw it in the garbage," Nurse Bessie threatened, as she peeped her head in the door.

"I'm scared. I want my mother," I cried.

"There ain't no Robin in here. You will obey or be punished. Stop all that damn crying," Nurse Bessie said again.

I didn't say another word. She didn't realize how scared I was. When she left, I began crying again. This time, a male staff member came to check on me.

"Are you okay in here?" he asked.

"I'm scared. I want my mother," I replied, as I sat up in bed.

"Nurse Bessie said she told you there is no mother. There is no one coming to rescue you, so it's best to stop all that crying," he answered.

"Okay."

"I'm Nurse Tim."

"Okay."

Nurse Tim came into the room. He looked weird. He stared at me with a black belt in his hand.

"You've been mighty bad, disobeying Nurse Bessie. She doesn't like that, and neither do I. All this crying is keeping the others up. Take off your clothes," he demanded.

"For what?"

"Don't question me, boy. Take off your clothes."

"No."

"You will do as I tell you."

"No! I'm not taking off my clothes."

I jumped up and ran toward the door. Nurse Tim grabbed me and slammed me to the floor. I was out for a while. When I woke up, my behind was sore. I saw Nurse Tim pulling up his pants. I had terrible pain there. He walked out, and I was bent over the bed with my pants down to my knees.

The next night, I didn't cry. Nurse Bessie stood at the door and looked at me with a mean face. "Don't start no trouble tonight, Dune."

"Can I get some water?" I asked.

"There ain't no water. Take your ass to sleep," she ordered.

"But I'm thirsty."

"What did I say? You will get some water tomorrow."

I laid back down and went to sleep. I had made up my mind to fight. Maybe I could get what I wanted. That night was good except when Nurse Tim came around. His lustful ways made me uneasy. I know he had sex with me. Robin always expressed to me to not like anyone touch my private. Nurse Tim touched my private. I needed to tell someone.

A couple of days later, I saw the doctor. He was rude and nasty to me. I was just a child, and he didn't care. He was white and saw me as a monster. Just because I was biracial didn't mean I was a monster.

"Your family is supposed to be here, but they aren't. I wonder why that is," he stated, as he frowned at me.

"My mother and John will come for me."

"Your mother and John will come here to help answer questions about your past. They won't be taking you anywhere."

"Why not? I haven't done anything."

"You did do something. Did you forget?"

"I was hungry."

"Well, you being hungry got you in here. You don't eat other people, just food."

"I know, but I couldn't help it."

That was the first time I had that craving for my favorite meat. I smelled the doctor, and he reeked of cigars. That made me sick.

"This stage in your stay here is the intake process. Do you understand what that means?"

"No, I don't."

Suddenly, Robin showed up. She looked like an old run-down woman. Her clothes were shabby. Her hair looked wild.

"I'm here. Let's get this over with," she shot.

"Welcome. I'm going to be Reagus Dune's doctor. I'm Steven Smith," he introduced himself to Robin.

"I'm Robin, this psycho's mother. What do I need to do?"

"First, you must answer a few questions."

"What are the questions?"

"Mother, I want to go home," I stated with tears falling down my face.

"You won't be going home anytime soon. Look what you have done. You have the KKK coming around, trying to find you. I know you're just a child but look at all the trouble you have brought to yourself," Robin explained.

"I still want to go home with you."

"Reagus, you have to understand why you're here," Dr. Steven Smith stated. He continued, "May I call you Robin?"

"Sure. Hurry up. I have somewhere to be," Robin shot off.

"We did an intake process already when you first brought him here, it states in the records. That was the initial therapy session. I want to learn about you and the relationship you have with your child."

"What relationship? He's my son, and that's it."

"I need to establish a connection with your child."

"Go ahead and talk to him, not me."

"Reagus, do you know why you are here?" Dr. Steven Smith asked.

"Yes, I bit a girl's leg because I was hungry."

"How long have you been coping with this problem of eating people?"

"I don't know. I just want to eat."

"If I gave you food, would you still want to eat people?

"Yes, it tasted so good."

"See, I told you he was a psycho," Robin yelled out.

"He's not a psycho but a confused child.

"Have you ever thought about harming other people or yourself?"

"What?" I asked.

"Do you want to eat other people?" Robin yelled out.

"Yes, I do, but I know it's wrong."

"I'm not taking this little bastard with me. He might try to eat me," Robin stated.

Suddenly, I jumped up and began attacking Robin. She fell to the ground, and I was trying to bite her. Not to eat but to kill her. Dr. Steven. Smith tried to get me off her. He immediately called for help. Two nurses came in and got me off Robin.

"You little shit, I'm going to kill you," Robin threatened, as she tried to reach me.

A nurse got in between us. I began attacking her. I was biting her arm, as blood came out, running down the side of my mouth. The male nurse pulled me away with a chunk of her meat in my *mouth. I chewed it up and spit it out. Her skin was nasty.*

"Restrain him immediately!" Dr. Steven Smith yelled out.

The female nurse was screaming, holding her arm. I was in attack mode. The male nurse had a hard time holding me down. Another male nurse showed up and sedated me. I was out like a light.

Every night, I was in attack mode. They had to put me in a straitjacket and lock me down in a white padded room. I was out of control. My mind was on its own. Nobody was safe from my wrath.

One night, it was colder than many other nights. I sat there with this straitjacket on, looking all crazy. The padded door opened, and Nurse Ben and Nurse Jacob stepped in.

"Are you ready to eat, my little cannibal?" Nurse Ben joked.

"He hasn't eaten in days. He should be," Nurse Jacob replied.

"I don't see how the kid can survive. It's been what, two days now?"

"Yep, since yesterday evening."

"Yes, I'm hungry," I replied with a soft voice.

"Don't 'yes, I'm hungry' in no soft voice to me. You going to have to man up in here," Nurse Ben stated, as he walked over and helped me to my feet.

"Be easy, Ben. He's just a kid."

"A kid in a straitjacket. He's in here for a reason."

"I guess."

"Think about it. You read the chart."

"That chart says a child was acting up."

"Don't forget biting folks."

"Okay, biting people and had to be locked up. Okay, I admit it's not normal to eat people. It's not normal to want to eat people," Nurse Jacob stated.

"I know."

"I'm hungry. Can I eat now?" I said with a little more bass in my voice.

"Sure, let's go, and don't try no funny stuff," Nurse Ben said, as he directed me outside of the door.

They had a chair there to sit me down in, and Nurse Jacob fed me. He was kind and very thoughtful, but Nurse Ben was harsh with a nasty attitude, just like Nurse Bessie.

"Hurry up feeding this animal. I need to teach him a lesson," Nurse Ben said.

"Leave him alone. He's just a kid."

"We have to break them in before they start with the bullshit," Nurse Ben stated.

"I don't care. Leave him alone."

"I will this time," Nurse Ben replied.

After my feeding, they locked me back down in the padded cell. It seemed like the straitjacket was too tight. I needed out.

"Help. Help. Help," I screamed.

Rushing to the door was Nurse Ben. "What do you want?"

"I can't breathe in this thing. I'm dying."

"You're not dying. You just have to get used to it."

"Let me out of this mutherfucking jacket. You hear me?" I yelled with force.

"No, I won't let you out that mutherfucking jacket, you fucking animal," Nurse Ben repeated after me.

"Fuck you, fuck you. You better let me out. I can't fucking breathe," I yelled.

"I'm going to quiet you right now."

He fumbled around with the keys and opened the door. He approached me, tugging at the front of my pants. I began trying to kick him but failed. I couldn't do much without my arms.

"You fucking idiot, I'm going to teach you a lesson."

"Help. Help. Help," I called out again.

Nurse Jacob rushed in and saw Nurse Ben over me. Nurse Jacob stepped out and closed the door. Nurse Ben continued to undo my pants. I was hurting before, but now, it was worse. I was awake to experience everything. Every thrust, every stroke.

After he finished with me, he pulled up my pants and left me there, crying. I was just a kid at the time. That day, I vowed to seek revenge on him and his family. I would find out whatever it was to hurt him – anything – and Nurse Jacob would be punished too.

A year passed by, and Nurse Ben came in every other night and deposited himself into me. It hurt, but I got used to it. Robin or John didn't come to visit me. I wanted to tell her what this man was doing to me, but she never showed. I told Dr. Steven Smith, but he didn't believe me. After I kept telling them repeatedly, they finally put me in a room with a camera. After a few times with the camera, Nurse Ben was fired, and charges were filed through the state. Robin showed up because she thought she was getting some money.

A few years passed, and it was my sixteenth birthday. I had gotten out a couple of times to be with the rest of the boys until I started biting them. But today, I was locked down. I had bitten too many people. They decided to keep me locked in for a year.

One hot night, I was preyed upon by Nurse Bessie and Nurse Tim. I screamed and screamed until someone came to the door to see what was wrong with me.

"Are you crazy, Dune? Why are you doing all this screaming, keeping the rest of the boys awake?" Nurse Tim asked.

"I need some water; my throat is dry. I need some water."

"If I give you some water, will you shut up?"

"Yes, I will be quiet. It's just that I'm thirsty. Must have been that cake Nurse Bessie cooked for me," I stated.

"Okay, but don't try anything. I hate to be telling your mother why I beat the hell out of you, killing you," Nurse Tim threatened.

"I'm not trying anything with you."

Nurse Tim gave me some water and walked out. I didn't bother to do anything. I was happy that someone cared about my birthday. Nurse Bessie was a mean old woman, and I liked her. She was like a mother figure to me until…

One stormy night, she turned into the devil. The thunder was rumbling so loud it could be heard from miles away. I was kicking the walls and raising hell. I wanted out of that straitjacket. There was no way they could keep me in here like this.

"Let me the fuck out of here. Hey, you! Let me out."

"Dune, don't start no mess tonight. I'm tired and need rest. You need to sit down somewhere," Nurse Bessie stated to me.

"Sit down somewhere or what? What will you do to me, you old hag?" I laughed.

"There's a lot I could do to you, so you need to watch your mouth. I'm not in the mood."

"I'm not in the mood either. Let me get out of this damn jacket. Y'all can't do this to me."

"We aren't doing nothing to you; you're doing it all by yourself."

"Let me out, old hag."

"Tim, bring the pliers."

"What do you need with pliers? You better not touch me, or I'll kill you and everybody in here."

"How are you going to do that with a straitjacket on?" she asked.

"I'll figure something out. You better not come near me."

"Or what?"

"Here are the pliers," Nurse Tim said with a dirty look on his face. His grin was sneaky, and I didn't like the look.

"Open the door," she ordered.

"Yes, ma'am," Nurse Tim said with happiness.

As soon as he opened the door, he kicked me in my chest, sending me to the padded floor.

"What the fuck?" I got out of my mouth before he kicked me repeatedly.

"You shouldn't be a disobedient little bastard. Some of this shit you brought on yourself."

"You can't do this shit to me."

"Yes, the fuck I can and will."

"No cursing, Tim," Nurse Bessie stated, as she positioned the pliers. She continued, "Hold him down, Tim."

Nurse Tim climbed on top of me, putting pressure on my chest, but not enough that I couldn't breathe.

"Get off me, you sick fuck," I said, squirming, as Nurse Tim sat down a little harder. I continued, "I can't breathe. I can't breathe."

"Hold up, Tim. Don't sit too hard on the boy and kill him. I just want him to shut up all that darn screaming."

"Me too. You got the needle."

"Get off me before I tell on you too. I'll get you fired," I screamed.

"You'll think twice before you rat on us," Nurse Bessie threatened.

Before I could say anything else, Nurse Bessie tried to grab my tongue. I bit down on the pliers. She pulled them out fast, causing one of my teeth to fall out. Screaming out, she grabbed my tongue with the pliers, almost pulling it from my head. Nurse Tim grabbed the pliers, and she pulled a plastic packet from her pocket.

"Are you going to do it this time?" Nurse Tim asked. He continued, "Remember, you stopped on the last boy. I want to see you go through with it, or I will stop helping you," he threatened.

"Don't you threaten me, boy."

"I'm not threatening you. I'm just saying. Here we are again, I need to see results."

"And results I shall give you."

Nurse Bessie took out a small needle and began sticking it in my tongue. I screamed with agony. She took it out and stuck me again. My eyes were trying to focus on the needle and her hand. I could see blood on the needle, and she kept penetrating me with it. Tears formed in my eyes and ran down my face. I tried screaming louder and louder, but it fell on a deaf ear.

"That's enough," Nurse Bessie spoke.

"Leave the needle in his tongue until in the morning. I bet he won't be screaming all night as always."

"I think he's had enough."

"You only stuck him a couple of times."

"Let me do it. I will make sure he won't scream all night," Nurse Tim replied with excitement.

"Here."

Nurse Tim took the pliers from Nurse Bessie. It seemed like her grip was harder than his. He took the needle and rammed it into my tongue over and over until blood almost covered his hand. Nurse Bessie turned her head, not wanting to look at me. I pierced his face, trying to get him to stop.

"Stop it, Tim. Look at all this blood. How in the world are we going to explain this? You need to clean this mess up," she remarked.

"I was going to keep going. Are you not tired of hearing him scream all night?" he asked, as he was about to penetrate my tongue again with the needle.

"Don't do it anymore. That's enough. Clean up," she ordered.

"You are ending my fun," he said.

Nurse Bessie looked into my eyes and let my tongue go. I screamed a low cry, as the two cleaned up everything. My tongue was on fire. In my head, I was killing them. I didn't know how I was going to do it, but they both had to die. Just like Nurse Ben and Nurse Jacob, they both had to die.

Months passed by before I could talk again. Dr. Steven Smith didn't know why I stopped talking. Debra Ebo, a social worker, had come into play. Nobody could get me to talk until my mouth was well. It was kind of a good thing because I came out of the straitjacket.

I experienced so much with Nurse Bessie. One quiet, hot night, I was asleep in my bed when Nurse Tim and Nurse Bessie walked through the door.

"Why weren't you at church services this morning?" Nurse Bessie asked.

"I was asleep and didn't hear them announce it," I replied, half asleep. I continued, "Plus I didn't want to go. The church is boring to me, and that's for the younger kids."

"Church is for everyone, and you need to start going," Nurse Bessie stated.

"Why? It's just church. And I've never been to church before. Robin didn't allow me to attend."

"You've been in here for years now. You know church services are every Sunday," Nurse Tim stated, as he approached me with a leather belt in his hand.

"And what do you think you're going to do with that?" I asked.

"I'm about to beat your ass. You know better than to not attend church."

"You need to be punished," Nurse Bessie remarked.

Before I could say another word, Nurse Tim started beating me with the belt. I grabbed the belt, and he began fighting me like a man. I began fighting him back harder than I ever had. Nurse Bessie took the belt and began hitting me so hard. Nurse Tim was fighting me hard.

I stopped fighting and folded up like a baby. Nurse Bessie beat me and recited a prayer. After it was over, I was bruised and hurt. I couldn't fight

Nurse Tim off me. I probably could have if Nurse
Bessie wasn't beating me with her belt.

****

Dr. Amanda Smith asked, "So, you experienced all this in there?"

"Yes, I did. There is more, but I won't get into details," I responded.

The psychiatrist looked at me with a puzzled look on her face. She wanted me to tell her more, but I just couldn't.

"Why not?" Dr. Smith asked. "Why didn't you report any of this stuff?"

"I did report it to Dr. Stephen Smith, but he didn't believe me."

"You couldn't have told someone else about the situation?

"Tell them what? I didn't want to be punished anymore. I could tell you so much more that happened to me. There was me being beaten on the bottom of my feet, them trying to pull my teeth to keep from biting the staff, and so on."

"Why commit the crime if you knew you were going to be punished?"

"I was crazy and didn't give a fuck about the punishment until they did it," I responded.

"That's crazy," she replied, as she shook her head.

"I am what I am, and nobody can change that."

"What are you – a serial killer, psycho, psychopath, or what?" Dr. Amanda Smith asked.

"I'm none of those. I'm Reagus Dune."

After she asked me all those questions, we sat there in silence for a few minutes until she started back up with more crazy shit.

CHAPTER 12

(Fuck Your Feelings, No Remorse)

Dr. Amanda Smith asked, "Have you ever experienced any happiness?"

"I have to say when Joyce told me she was pregnant. I couldn't believe I was going to be a father to a child. I wondered how the hell I was going to take care of a child with no job. That's another reason why I started working at the doctor's office in Decatur. There were other happy moments, but that was my happiest," I replied.

Occurred Incident: HAPPINESS

As a child, I experienced an unbelievable thing. Robin and John thought they were too high to see what they saw. I was confused and left alone for a whole weekend by myself. No food, no water, no bath, or no grooming.

Sleeping, my stomach began to bother me. It was cramping and bubbling at the same time. I wanted to tell Robin, but she would have slapped the mess out of me and told me to go back to bed. Sitting straight up in the bed, I began vomiting on the bed then the floor. I started screaming out, pulling seaweed from my mouth. Robin opened the door abruptly.

"What the hell is going on with you, boy?" she asked.

"Help me. Something is wrong with me," I responded.

Suddenly, I started pulling seaweed from me. It was long.

"What the hell?" John said, as he stood in the doorway.

My legs began to crack. Bones were breaking at the joints. It started with my legs, then my ankles, and elbows. I screamed out for Robin, but she just stood there in disbelief. I was laying on the bed with broken bones.

"Help me," I screamed, as Robin did nothing.

Suddenly, I sat up in bed, and my head turned, while I was talking in another language.

"This some TV shit," John said. He continued, *"Let's get the hell out of here."*

All you could hear was bones breaking. My eyes turned black as night. Robin entered the room.

"Get your ass back here. Something is wrong with that kid."

"I can't just leave him. He's my child."

John entered the room. Suddenly, something pushed him and Robin back out the bedroom door. It was like the wind took them by surprise. Nails started flying out of nowhere. One hit John in the shoulder. Another passed Robin's face. The picture *of Jesus on the wall was hit with nails. The cross on the wall turned backward.*

Robin and John quickly exited the apartment. My door was bolted shut with nails. I was still speaking another language. My screams rang out. I woke up to find Robin and John gone. I was alone in the apartment.

A few days later, Robin and John returned to the apartment. Both feared me.

"Reagus, are you alright?" Robin yelled from afar. She said again, "Reagus, are you alright?"

"Reagus," John yelled out.

I walked out the bedroom door with no problem. My bones weren't broken. My head was on correctly. And I didn't speak another language. I was a normal kid. Why were they acting afraid of me? It was only a dream, my dream.

"I'm hungry," I spoke, as I walked toward Robin.

"I will fix your something to eat."

John kept staring at me. He looked at his shoulder, but nothing was there. There was no nail stuck in his shoulder. He was okay. All I could remember was Robin leaving me for the weekend and returning on Sunday.

After that day, Robin was a mother for once. She dressed me for school and fed me well. I was living a good life. I enjoyed her for the short time she was normal.

"Reagus Dune, get your butt in here," Robin yelled out.

"Yes," I said.

"I told you to clean this house up. Why is it still dirty? Look at these clothes everywhere. Look at this mess."

"I don't remember you asking me to clean up."

"Don't you be a smart ass."

"I don't remember."

Robin grabbed a belt, beating me so hard it left whelps everywhere. The next day I went to school and bit into Bonnie Logan. She smelled so good that I couldn't resist. After that day, I was tossed into the asylum.

SECOND INCIDENT

Joyce and I exited the East Central bus at Vowell's. She was very quiet and distant that day. I figured maybe she was on her period or something. They say women experienced so many things.

"What's wrong with you? You have been quiet and not speaking to me all day," I asked, as I reached for her, and she pulled back.

"I'm not in the mood for your bullshit today. No, I don't want to laugh. I don't want to do

*anything but go home and sleep," Joyce replied
with an attitude.*

*"I wasn't going to make you laugh this time.
I want to know what is wrong with you."*

"Go away, Reagus."

*"Okay, I will. I don't need your attitude
today either."*

"Bye."

*"Bye," Joyce spoke, as she turned to walk
off and then turned back around. She continued, "I
have something to tell you, but I don't know how
you're going to take it."*

*"Say it. I can take it if you have another
man."*

"That's not it."

*"Are you sure because you have been
treating me like crap."*

"I'm pregnant," Joyce blurted out.

"Pregnant."

*"Yes. My mother wants me to get an
abortion, but I refuse to. I want someone to love and
that person to love me back. I want this baby,"
Joyce stated.*

*"Maybe your mother is right. I don't know
how to raise a baby, and you don't either," I
replied, but deep down, I was happy.*

*"You're just like her. My baby is a human,
not just some animal you put down. Reagus, you*

don't have to be involved in my baby's life. I will take care of him or her by myself."

"Joyce, I'm sorry. I didn't mean to sound like an asshole."

"Well, you did."

"I wouldn't know where to start raising a child. I'm already having issues with Robin. Then, I must take care of Kale and Kyle," I stated.

"You do know how to take care of a child. Kale and Kyle aren't grown. They are children."

"I know that. I'm talking about a baby."

"What about Amber Rose? She's a baby."

"I didn't think about that. You're correct."

"So, don't give me that I don't know how to take care of a baby crap," Joyce shot back.

"I'll be there for you. I'm happy anyway." I laughed.

"Reagus, you play too much."

"I got you though. I'm happy and will take care of you and our baby. We're graduating next month. I already work at the shelter, and I have an interview with Forest Medical Clinic. Don't worry. You will be taken care of," I promised, as we hugged.

A few months passed, and Joyce went into labor. I was scared to death. I had Kale and Kyle with me. I didn't want to leave them at home with Robin's crazy self. She would probably pawn them off if she could.

Kale and Kyle were barely awake.

"Kale, I need to go to the back with Joyce and the baby."

Peeping into the room, Joyce was in bed, and the baby was on some type of iron-looking bed with a warm light.

"About time you come and checked on me. You missed the delivery," Joyce said angrily.

"I couldn't come in."

"You knew I was having this baby."

"It doesn't matter; I am here now. I have been here the whole time, just not in the delivery room," I replied. I didn't want to smell all that blood. Joyce was already smelling good enough for me to eat. I didn't want to have a reason to kill her. She was smelling loud, and I had to control myself.

"Is it a girl or a boy?" I asked, as I tiptoed toward the crib.

"He's a boy."

"Awesome."

"I'm naming him Brady."

"Why Brady? Just name him after me."

"Remember, you go by Reagus Benton in public, Reagus Dune in private. How would I do that? Robin has given you a whole new identity."

"You're right. But I came around to being myself. I hate that Robin did that, but I know her reason," I spoke, as I rubbed my head.

"Don't worry. I will give him my last name." Joyce stated.

"Okay," I agreed, as I picked up Brady and held him for the first time. He didn't have a smell to him at all. I was happy about that because I didn't want to kill him.

****

Dr. Amanda Smith asked, "So, why did you let them live that hurt you at the East Mississippi Mental Institution? Nurse Bessie? Nurse Tim? Nurse Ben? Nurse Jacob?"

"Who said I let them live? Maybe they just haven't been found. And please don't forget about Dr. Steven Smith. He didn't believe what all they were doing to me in that awful place."

"So, you're trying to say that Dr. Steven Smith has died too?" Dr. Amanda Smith asked.

"That's exactly what I am saying," I replied with no remorse.

Occurred Incident: *NURSE BESSIE AND NURSE TIM'S DEATH*

It was dusk dark outside; I walked up to Nurse Bessie's house. I parked my car down the street, so nobody would notice it when I made my exit. Slowly stepping up the stairs, the house was very quiet. I was nervous as hell because Nurse Tim had been there for over two hours now. I knew they were having an affair because I overheard them talk about it in the mental institution. I took the 12-gauge shotgun out from under my trench coat and had on my backpack full of goodies. Searching for the spare key under the flowerpot by the door, I retrieved it and unlocked the door.

Walking slowly through the house with my 12-gauge ready to shoot, I overheard Nurse Bessie moaning and screaming out. These two were having sex. Even better for me. My plan was to torture these two mutherfuckers like they did me. Whichever was quicker.

Slowly stepping up to the door, it had a crack in it. Nurse Tim was on top of Nurse Bessie, giving her old ass the business. I opened the door, and it gave out this loud screeching noise. I raised my 12-gauge.

"What's up, bitch?" I yelled, as I raised my 12-gauge shotgun and blasted him in the back.

He fell over, screaming. Nurse Bessie was screaming.

"Please don't kill me, don't kill me!" Nurse Bessie yelled.

"Shut the fuck up," I yelled out.

"What do you want with me?" Nurse Bessie asked, as fear showed on her face.

"Help me! Help me!" Nurse Tim called out.

He wasn't dead. He was reaching for something, but before I could react, he pulled out a gun from under the pillow and shot toward me. He hit me once on the shoulder. I ran down the hall into the living room. The house was dark, and I was unfamiliar. I heard them from down the hall. I had to do something quick.

"Call the fucking police! Hurry up!" Nurse Tim called out.

"I can't. The phone is in the kitchen on the counter," she yelled out.

"Fuck. Stay here. I'm going to go get it," Nurse Tim ordered.

"No, don't leave me. He's still in the house," she stated.

"He's probably gone; I hit that mutherfucker," he replied.

"It looked like Reagus Dune," Nurse Bessie said.

"Who?" he asked.

"The boy from the mental institution. Reagus Dune! Remember the needle in the tongue. Pulling the tooth," she explained.

"Shit, he's out?" Nurse Tim asked.

"That's who it looked like to me."

"Okay, let's calm down and move together. Just always stay behind me," Nurse Tim demanded.

"Okay." She complied.

*I heard them coming down the hall. They
turned on the light in the hallway. Nurse Tim had
the gun sticking out. Nurse Bessie was holding onto
his shirt. As soon as I saw him enter the living
room, I hit him and knocked the gun from his hand.
We began fighting. Nurse Bessie ran straight to the
kitchen for the house phone. I beat Nurse Tim down
badly. He just lay there. I grabbed my 12-gauge
shotgun and went to the kitchen.*

*"I have an intruder. I think his name is
Reagus..." Nurse Bessie trailed off.*

*I blasted her in the face, causing her head to
split open. The phone dropped to the ground. I
could hear the 911 dispatcher still talking. Her
body just fell over like a sack of potatoes. I walked
back over to Nurse Tim; he was laying there,
moaning. I took out my knife and cut his throat. I
thought blood was going to squirt in my face, but it
didn't. Blood oozed from his neck. I hurried up and
got out of there. By this time, I could hear police
sirens. Exiting the house, leaving the front door
wide open, I dashed down the street with the 12-
gauge shotgun hidden in my trench coat. As the
police car passed, I ducked by a car.*

*Finally, I got to my car and drove away. I
went home and nursed the bullet wound I had. As
least the bullet went straight through. That shit
hurt. I had an open wound in my back, but I sewed
the front up with needle and thread. I kept rubbing*

alcohol on it, so it wouldn't get infected. After about two months, it healed. I was happy about that. I wouldn't make that mistake again.

Occurred Incident: NURSE BEN'S DEATH

Crouching down behind Nurse Ben's car for a long time had my back hurting. I had to pee. My eyes were getting heavy. I was bored. I was tired of playing with the taser in my hand. Nurse Ben was either going to work late, or he wasn't going at all. If he wasn't going to work, then I would have to come up with a new plan. I would have to break in and murder his punk ass just like I did with Nurse Bessie and Nurse Tim.

As soon as my thoughts were about to consume me, he exited his house. He had on some Beats headphones. I was behind his car. He hit the remote start on his truck, turning it on, then turned around, heading back into the house.

"Dammnit," I whispered to myself. The truck had those loud pipes. The neighbors probably looked out the window. Hopefully, this would be peaceful. Suddenly, he came out the door again, this time with a bookbag in his hand. I was praying a kid didn't come out behind him. He opened the truck door, and before he could get in, I hit him with the taser right in his neck. He fell out but was not knocked out. Grabbing his body and dragging him back to the front door, I took his keys and

opened the front door. It took me a minute or two to find the key. I saw he was coming back around; I hit him again with the taser and then again.

Pulling his body into the house, I closed the door behind us. Taking out my knife from my bookbag I had on, I stabbed that asshole in his stomach twice. He curled up in a knot.

"Please don't kill me. I have kids," Nurse Ben begged.

"You should have thought about your kids before you raped me," I shot back.

"Reagus!" he blurted out.

"The one and only."

"Reagus, please forgive me. I didn't mean to hurt you. I was young and dumb," he explained, as he held his stomach.

"I don't want to hear your excuses now. You should have thought about that a long time ago," I replied.

"Please don't kill me," he begged.

"I WAS ONLY A CHILD!" I screamed.

"I know, and that's why I ask you to forgive me," he stated.

"Forgive this," I replied, as I jumped down on him and began beating him. I hit him repeatedly with my fists until he passed out.

I began taking off his pants. I got a chair and some rope from my bag. Struggling to tie him to the chair, I did it. Lifting Nurse Ben and the chair, I pushed it against the wall with his head touching the wall. His ass was exposed, naked. Getting my Gorilla Tape, I was ready to tape his mouth shut. I listened for his truck to shut off, and it did. If you hadn't moved it in fifteen minutes or so, it would shut off on its own. Hopefully, none of his nosey neighbors saw me.

As he woke up, I spoke, "Are you ready for me?"

"What are you doing? Where are my pants? Untie me right now!" Nurse Ben ordered.

"Which one do you want me to do first? Untie you or give you your pants? Which one is it?" I laughed.

"Bitch, stop playing with me. Untie me from this fucking chair right now," he demanded.

"Well, I'm not doing either one, but you can take this," I spoke, as I stuck my penis in his ass, and he screamed like a hog. He bucked and bucked in the chair, as I pumped and pumped.

"Reagus, please stop," Nurse Ben begged.

"Nope," I replied, as I kept going, and he was bracing himself.

I didn't finish; I just stopped. I wasn't feeling right. Not having sex with no man.

"You took my manhood from me. You knew you were wrong. How could you have sex with little kids?" I asked.

"Reagus, please don't do this. I apologized for what I had done to you."

"Your apology means nothing to me. So, how many kids have you done this to?" I asked him, hoping he would say that I was the only one. But...

"I don't know. Just untie me," he answered.

"What you mean you don't know?" I replied with a little anger.

"I don't know how many."

I walked to my bookbag, took my knife back out, and cut the rope. He fell off the chair onto the floor. I jumped down on him and began stabbing him repeatedly until I was tired, and the knife broke into his eye socket. He was a bloody mess. I was a bloody mess. I didn't know how many times I stabbed that weak ass punk. He made me just that angry. When they heard of his death, all of those he raped would be happy. I stood up, and my knees were weak. I pulled off my clothes and put them in my bookbag. I took a quick shower and got some of his clothes and put them on. They were a little bit baggy on me.

Walking back into the living room, Nurse Ben lay there, dead. I took the shirt back out of the bag and grabbed the blade from Nurse Ben's eye socket, pulling it out. Stuffing everything into my bookbag, I was ready to go. Exiting the house, the neighbor across the street was out. He was outside in the trunk of his car. I pulled down my hat close to my eyes and walked down the street.

Occurred Incident: NURSE JACOB'S DEATH

It was kind of hard to catch Nurse Jacob by himself. One of his friends was always with him or one of his girlfriends. He didn't have any kids. He lived in an apartment building where you had to check in with the guard at the front desk. When he came out at night to get in the car from work, it would always be four or five of them at one time.

I trailed Nurse Jacob and one of his girlfriends from this nightclub at one in the morning in a stolen vehicle. We got up on the interstate; he was driving fast, in and out of traffic, in his new Dodge Challenger. Traffic began to slow down, and I hurried up, getting behind him. As he got off the interstate, so did I. I passed him, and he passed me back. I guess he called himself racing me. I wasn't about to bring attention to myself; then again, I did start it. I got up beside him, revving the motor to my vehicle, Ready to take off. He took off like a bat out of hell. I took off behind him, hoping the Glock 45 didn't fall off the passenger seat. I had to grab it and stick it between the seats.

As we got down in the residential area, we didn't race anymore. We just cruised. I ran into the back of his Challenger on purpose. Grabbing the

Glock 45, I was ready. He didn't get out at first, then he jumped out.

"You hit my fucking car. What the fuck is wrong with you?" he yelled.

"My bad, man," I spoke out, as I jumped out and put six bullets in his chest.

His body fell backwards, as I ran back to the vehicle. I could hear the girl in the car screaming. Lights were coming on inside houses. I got the hell out of there quickly. It didn't take me long to get back up on the interstate. I was hoping he was dead. I didn't have time to make sure but them six bullets to his chest should make sure. Four down and one more to go was all I could think of.

Occurred Incident: DR. STEVEN SMITH'S DEATH

Watching Dr. Smith and his friends, Henry and Carl, pack for a hunting trip outside his house made me feel uneasy. I didn't know how in the world I was going to slip up on the three of them. All three of them together were much stronger than me, but that was okay because I had my Nosler Black Bolt Action Rifle with my Vortex Viper PST Gen II Rifle Scope with me. I had been carrying it around with me ever since I learned of this so-called hunting trip. Dr. Smith didn't even seem like the type to hunt. He was just out of shape to me, but who knows? He never exercised. I had been following him for a while now, and it was time for him to die.

Leaving out of the driveway, I trailed him and his friends to this campground. I stayed my distance to keep from being noticed. Nobody was at the campground but them, so I know I couldn't park my car there. I waited until they unloaded their car and disappeared into the woods before I approached their car. Flattening all four tires, I put the rifle over my shoulders and proceeded into the woods. I had to make sure not to run up on them idiots. Hopefully, they wouldn't kill me before I killed them.

Coming up on their deer stand, I moved back a little farther and laid down with my rifle aimed directly at the deer stand. I fixed my scope to focus directly on the stairs leading up and down the deer stand. I just might pick them off one by one, as they came down, then again, I didn't know.

I laid down on the ground for so long that I thought I fell asleep. Suddenly, I heard movement. Looking up, Henry was damn near up on me. I had to lay very still, and he released himself on the ground. As he zipped up his pants, I adjusted my rifle and aimed. BANG! I shot, splitting his head in two. His body fell to the ground gently. I repositioned myself before the other two came out. The shot was very loud.

The two climbed down the ladder and started walking around the deer stand.

I just stared at the two for a few seconds, walking closer to them.

Before they could react, I lifted my rifle and shot Carl right between the eyes. His head split open, and blood splashed in Dr. Smith's face. Carl's body fell like a sack of potatoes. Dr. Smith yelled out and took off running. I loaded my rifle, walking behind him. He was getting a little distance between us, so I took off running behind him.

Catching up to him, I shot and hit him in the leg. He fell. He got back up and began limping.

"You should have believed me when I told you what they did to me in that awful place, Dr. Smith," I stated, as I walked behind him.

I continued, "They hurt me; they hurt me bad. And you stood by, doing nothing."

He stopped and turned around, saying, "Reagus Dune."

"The one and only. You let them hurt me. I was just a child. It's funny that you remembered that I am the one you let them hurt," I spoke.

"You had no proof," he replied.

"I was just a child. You should have had me checked out. I told you that monster raped me. But later when you put that camera in my room, you found out it was true. You fired him, but you didn't

give me any counseling or medical care," I continued to say.

"You were just fine. You seem to be alright," he spoke.

"I still needed help. HE HURT ME," I yelled, as I held up the rifle and put a bullet in his shoulder. He squealed out like a hog.

"I should have helped you. Please don't kill me. I have a family. My kids," he explained.

"They pulled my tooth with pliers, stuck a needle in my tongue, almost breaking my leg. I could go on and on, but I won't. You deserve to die. Therefore, I sentence you to death."

"Reagus, no, please," Dr. Smith begged.

I shot him right between the eyes, causing his head to explode since I was in close range. I shot him dead in the heart because my heart ached because of all the stuff he let them do to me. Afterwards, I walked off, leaving his dead body right there on the ground. Somebody would find him one day. If not, then so be it. Maybe the animals would gnaw on him. All I knew was that I got my revenge.

CHAPTER 13

(Game Over)

Dr. Amanda Smith (Psychiatrist): Execution Day for Reagus Dune.

Dr. James Bryant sat across the table from me. He was the last psychiatrist I saw. It had been a couple of weeks since I had been coming to his office. I didn't know what happened to Dr. Amanda Smith. I heard she had gone crazy after conversations with me.

"Do you think you did the right thing?" Dr. Bryant asked, as he looked down at his notebook with a new ballpoint pen.

"Yes, I know I did the right thing. I didn't think the execution was going to go through because I am what they call mentally ill," I answered, as I lay on the sofa with my legs crossed.

"Technically, the execution was going to happen regardless."

"I understand that. I am happy with the decisions I made."

"You do understand why you are in here?"

"Yes, I understand why I'm in this nut house. Everybody knows that Reagus Dune was killed and is known as a serial killer. I killed hundreds. You act like you didn't know this."

"I'm just making sure because you don't seem to have no remorse that you killed. I'm trying to help your case, but you're making this hard for me."

"I don't care about all that. We have been over this time after time. I want to talk about something else. You talked about helping me with my case. Why? My execution will be in a few hours. I don't see why I am here talking to you."

"Okay, what do you want to talk about?" Dr. Bryant asked, as he put down the notebook and pen. He sat back in his chair, crossing his legs, as I sat up, looking directly at him.

"I don't know. Anything but Reagus Dune," I answered.

"You killed hundreds of people. What made you do that? You didn't eat them all, did you? You haven't answered any of my questions."

"Dr. Bryant, you already know the answer to these questions. We have gone over this repeatedly. I killed hundreds of people because I could do it. I wanted the police or FBI to track me down like how I hunted down my prey. Your answer is in everything I talked about. That lets me know that you're not listening to me," I remarked.

"You seem to be in your right mind about what you have done. You do know you're going to be executed."

"Yes, I do know I will be executed. To my understanding, you're not supposed to kill the mentally ill. That's what Dr. Amanda Smith told me."

"That may be true for the state of Mississippi."

"We all know I'm nuts. I love to eat people. That's not normal. I've had that craving since I was a child. The smell of different people made me go crazy. For example, you, Dr. Bryant, I wouldn't eat you at all. I would just kill you. Your skin doesn't smell good to me," I explained.

"So, you eat people if they have a certain smell?" he asked.

"I killed because I was hungry. You all go to the grocery store; I go to the streets," I spoke, as I looked back at Officer Keyes, who was standing guard with his hand on his gun, ready to put me down if I made a wrong move. I wasn't going to try anything. How could I in a mutherfucking straitjacket?

"What do you think I can do to help you?"

"I don't want no help. Just go ahead and execute me."

There was silence, as we both sat there.

DR. AMANDA SMITH'S CONFESSION

As other people and I sat quietly in a room with a window about to watch Reagus Dune get

executed, he smiled at all of us. He did not show
worry on his face, no remorse, nothing to show any
type of emotion. The officers prepared him for his
execution, and so many things were going through
my mind. He shouldn't die like this. He was
mentally ill and not just the cold-hearted killer that
the world saw him as.

Officer Keyes stood by, waiting for the say-
so to pull the handle on Reagus. Captain Dalton had
a smirk on his face. He was happy Dune was going
to die. All the crimes he committed were horrific.
So many red rock crape trees, weeping willow
shade trees, and yellow roses. I'd never seen so
many trees in one spot in my life.

Captain Dalton nodded his head to Officer
Keyes. Officer Keyes pulled the handle. Reagus
Dune's body started smoking, as he shook violently.
He was laughing and screaming like a madman. His
body went limp. Officer Keyes pulled the handle
back up. Captain Dalton went to check his pulse.
Reagus Dune came back to life, biting Captain
Dalton's wrist. Blood was everywhere. Officers
grabbed Captain Dalton quickly. Captain Dalton
nodded his head to Officer Keyes once again while
holding his wrist. The handle was pulled down
again, and Reagus Dune's body shook violently
again. You could hear what sounded like bones
cracking. His joints were breaking, and his limbs
were hanging from his body. He screamed louder,

as Officer Keyes held the handle down a little longer.

After a few minutes went by, everyone looked on, as Reagus Dune's head hung low. Captain Dalton had a handkerchief he wrapped his wrist in. Captain Dalton motioned for Officer Combs to check Reagus Dune's pulse. He backed away, shaking his hand. Captain Dalton motioned for Officer Keyes to check his pulse. Officer Keyes slowly walked over and checked his pulse.

"He's still breathing. That's impossible," Officer Keyes stated, as he moved back quickly.

"Smith, get over there and pull that handle again," Captain Dune ordered.

Suddenly, Reagus Dune's head lifted, as he smiled at us. His eyes turned as black as coal. The veins showed on his face, as he tried to talk. I jumped up, as Officer Smith pulled the handle again. Reagus Dune's body shook, as his eyes burst, and the veins popped through his skin. Officer Smith pulled the handle back down. This time, he barely lifted his head.

I rushed to the back, bursting the glass in the hallway to grab the axe. Running into the execution room, I walked slowly up to Reagus Dune, as blood dripped from his body. Lifting the axe, I decapitated his head clean from his body. This man was evil, and even an execution couldn't stop him. I had to do it. I had to be the one to kill Reagus Dune after he bit my leg back in elementary school. I had to play like I was Dr. Amanda Smith, the psychiatrist, to get close to him. I thought he was going to remember me from having sex with him at the shelter, but he didn't. I changed my hair color and appearance. That was the only way I could plot against Reagus Dune. That one bite had me traumatized. I had to see a psychiatrist and therapist just to get my mind right. Even though I was a little girl at the time, I couldn't forget what Reagus Dune had done to my life. My life was broken because of him. It stuck with me until my adulthood. I was broken, simple as that.

After I chopped off his head with an axe, officers rushed in to subdue me. It was crazy that in seconds, I became a killer. It didn't matter to me. I had to get even for what he did to me as a child. I was devastated for a long time. But I was happy because he was dead. He would no longer eat humans like animals. No more Monster. No more REAGUS DUNE.